HOW TO Succeed IN Love

The Enticing Love Story

DARIA SILVANO BRUCE

ISBN
978-1-956161-18-2 (Hardcover)
978-1-956161-17-5 (Paperback)
978-1-956161-16-8 (eBook)

To my one and only son and to the love of his life, my daughter- in-law, and to my three beautiful granddaughters, I love them very much. Without them, I would be lost. They are my inspiration.

To my two brothers and four sisters, to the love of their lives, to all my nieces and nephews, and to the rest in the immediate family circle, I love you, all.

In memoriam, a special dedication goes out to my departed loved ones: my husband, my parents, and my sister who never gave up on a tremendous fire (she died at the age of sixty-two). I miss you and I love you, all. May the Lord bless you and bring you, all, to the everlasting life.

To all the ones I loved before, to all my friends, and to all my relatives around the world. I love you, all.

I live loving you.

Thank you for loving me, as well.

————◖◗————

Table of Contents

You Mean to Tell Me That No One Has Ever Told You That I Love You? ... 1
Love Began When We Were Born.. 3
"You Know When the Opportunity Presents Itself, Say Yes." 5
Needless to Say, It Was Just a Very Hard Time 11
Ten Commandments of Love 17
A Significant Affair to Remember 23
I know both lovers' minds say 31
A question is asked 33
Kindness is best insurance of happiness................................... 35
Secret Love... 39
"Oh, yes! It's hot!" 43
Power & Magic of Love... 47
The Enticing Love Story 51
Summer Love... 53
"Just Like the Example About the Boat".................................... 57
Believe It or Not... 63
The Memories of Your Love Is Forever...................................... 65
Somewhere My Love 69
"That Made the Evening News on How to Succeed in Love." 75
Customer Imaginations Profile:.. 81
ADVICE!!!!! 83

You mean to tell me that no one has ever told you that I love you?

My lovers did, but I guess, I didn't believe it.

Did you know that the happiness of your love relationship depend, upon the quality of your thoughts; and that to be successful in love, always have to strive for perfection in everything you do? Remember, love really require attention. It doesn't mean that your partner is bad, or that he or she isn't a loving person. It means that through misunderstanding, the gravity of love will jump through the windows; and you will have misused the law of love.

If you believe that you are inferior to your lover, what was there!

In your mind that distracted you from being yourself?

For some reason, it hurts so much to separate myself from it.

It's because with that thing in mind, my lover and I are connected in love.

Perhaps no one realizes how important a good, healthy relationship is. It means love has grown stronger with every life you have lived and has truly been a lover's love. It means that two people not only love each other in that time, but also in all the other times. Just keep in mind that when the storm passes the sun appears.

What you are about to read in this book has the power to challenge and to change your love lifestyle. I have something to tell you about my secret (though not-so-secret-anymore) love story. Keep reading this book, and you just might find something interesting. Maybe you can change your outlook on love.

Love Began When
We Were Born

I was born in Talayong, Badian, in Cebu, an island in the Philippines. I live in an age when many of us have the same common, functional, standard family living. I am the fourth of seven children in my family, and ours was one full of loving happiness.

As my siblings and I grew older, my parents didn't want us to go anywhere else—especially to faraway places. It made them nervous because there were so many of us; however, I felt that I had to put my foot down, so I told them *"I love you, but we cannot live in this house forever."* My parents provided all of us a sense of belonging through service; and the sharing of love in our family circle's life gifted each of us faith, hope, and love. With all the love in my family while I was growing up, I learned to become a loving, independent teenager.

All of us in my family worked hard. My parents had a big farm on which they grew corn or any kinds of crops to eat. That farm provided my family a good living and sustained us in our daily lives.

My family was also in many ways resilient. Whenever we were faced with challenges, we simply found a solution in love. We were faithful to our parents, and they instilled in us an interest in farming. But at the time, I was interested in going to college; and it was then that I was in possession of a good ambition.

I found a job as a working student. I was sure that my parents could gave me the things that I wanted—especially if what I wanted was good education—but I thought, I love my parents very much. It's better to not lean on them for financial support, or else both of us will fall down.

With this, I demonstrated that familiar love is the most powerful force in the world. Believe me. I've found that this love had led me to appreciate the presence of my entire family. This presence of love is well expressed whenever we gather together as a family circle.

The meaning of love is the unity that brings people into our lives. We are the ones giving meaning to it. If you believe that you have expressed your love or understand your belief in your life, and if you believe that you have remained faithful in the law of love, then you can prove that you are open to the opportunity to develop your concept of love to the fullest.

You know that there is nothing too fair for a great deal of love. My parents are filled with love for us, their children, just like how their (our) forefathers—of all cultures and ages—dedicated themselves to building their own communities and their families' image of love.

"You know when the opportunity presents itself, say yes."

If you have the opportunity to take a chance in loving someone you're comfortable with, neutralize your ego to love yourself unconditionally.

Loving yourself does not bloat your ego because that's not what your ego is about. You have to take a chance on making your love life better. Truthful love shall be established to remain forever, but a dishonest love shall only last for a moment.

Not knowing the difference between these two types of love means: That you need to have a deeper understanding of love, if you believe that your success means you have complete control of love, then it also means that what was assumed to be true will become a reality.

At least, that's what I feel when I fall in love with somebody else. When love is new, it is great. There is so much more than just memories; for your love is forever, like all the evening stars embedded into the dark sky. When I look up and see Orion, the Big Dipper, Gemini, and the North Star (otherwise known as Polaris) twinkling, I am reminded of my enticing love story.

We came closer to each other. It felt almost wonderful as the morning drew near. The early mist hung in wet, green valleys under a beautiful bright-blue sky. All of it seemed as if to confirm that my wishes have come true: I found a new job and a new love. I thought that it was all a dream!

But it was true, and I thought that maybe it was the starting point of my life. And, I think, Yes, something that thrills or excites you, in your heart, you realize and see that it's the cherished dream of love.

I went to Cebu City to attend Southwestern University, where I studied for my bachelor's degree in the field of education. While I studied, I gave advice to many regarding romantic relationships, educated people on how to share their feelings with their loved ones, helped them to be more comfortable and eventually be successful in love.

I often told people "You must first make your life better. You must stand up for yourself when someone is putting you down. Do not think yourself unlovable when you end a bad relationship.

Take the risk even if you are afraid you will be hurt, but trust yourself to make the right decision. Have the courage to speak to stand up for your decision. If you think for yourself, you will come up with solutions to help yourself stand your ground and make the changes that are right for you in your love life.

In my experience, love can inspire each of us differently; but it's our ego that can trick us into believing that we're insecure, stupid, and unworthy. If you have ever felt this way, you are not alone. It doesn't matter what has happened in the past; you can change your love life if you choose to. You are never stuck with an old pattern, even if it seems your love life has been a disaster.

When I was still studying in college, I had the absolute responsibility for not only my education, but also for my love lifestyle. Though it wasn't ideal, I kept it secret because my parents were very old-fashioned and very strict. Needless to say, my parents didn't like that I had a boyfriend while I was still in school.

In fact, they gave me an ultimatum: stop seeing my boyfriend or stop going to school. So I had to choose between my schooling and my boyfriend, which at the time was extremely difficult for me. To make matters worse, my "boyfriend" was actually four different guys: Josh, Dr. Bob, Fred, and Lloyd, Each one shines in his own way; and they are all tall, dark, and handsome professionals. That made it even more difficult for me to make a decision.

It was sometime in college when I met someone online. My heart pounded every time I thought of those moments we talked about love.

Surely, that reaction is only natural. If you have the ability to seize the best opportunity to be highly successful in love, whether you take it or not, you will learn.

My heart felt such deep sorrow when I was made to choose between love and school by my parents; and education gave me happiness and a sense of accomplishment. But the truth is we're all self-made though in just different categories, even though the difference between each of us is not what ought to concern us—luck, the stars, fate, our parents; however, most people actually believe their love lives will be determined by chance, and I choose to think otherwise. I believe only lovers (the successful ones) understand. Fate merely gives us opportunities to experience love. The exciting relationships before are a little bit different from those of the younger generations today. Back then, one (usually the gentlemen) had to not only win the affections of the person they are besotted to, but also respect that person's parents and earn their trust (and evidently, their permission). The young lovers listened to the honest critiques from their parents and learned to appreciate the beauty of love in its simplest, purest form. But nowadays, as you can see, the young generation sweethearts often kiss openly in public places; but that is the custom now. In my time, I just followed the old-fashioned way. I don't know if the behaviors and expressions of love I'd employed before are the same as those in my parents' time. I mean, I did find the way that they treated my siblings and I while we were teenagers— especially when it came to relationships—so strict. The majority of parents before grossly underestimated their teenagers' ability to think, to act, to determine, and to shape their own futures to be better. They didn't like to see their own teenagers hugging and kissing in public. I have never tried to do this before; and I wonder if before the same rules applied to those of my age, or if they had to find the best place to show their affection to their special someone, and to give some respect to others. I knew they reaped and harvested their love and their capacity to think and to act. They are full of love, and that's just how it is.

I had a secret admirer when I was in my second year in college; but I put that aside and tried not to think about it because as I've said, my parents were very strict. They didn't want to see their teenage children kiss before they got married. So I tried to relax and convinced myself that

I didn't want to get involved into relationships yet (but mostly, I didn't want to get in trouble).

I was well loved by them, those four men; but I know we'd had these promises for far too long. If I continued my studies, I had to make sure that I don't entertain any more notions about having a boyfriend because if my parents knew about it, then I'd have to stop studying. I had to show them that I'd make good on my promise to focus on school.

It's been said that the couples go a long period of time without arguing and/or doubts about their relationship because both partners believe and trust each other. Yes, it's true. That's my answer. To experience this kind of love, I first had to have my happiness by following my road map to success and by earning all the things in life that I really wanted.

I had crawled through the road of my dreams; then one day, I heard somebody climbing up the stairs then knocking on my door. It was my girlfriend (and by "girlfriend," I mean female friend), and she came to ask me an unusual request. She said that she received a letter from her uncle Josh from Hawaii, and that she had to find a woman for him when he comes to visit in the Philippines.

After pondering on the situation introduced to me, I told her "I don't like that. I don't know him."

She replied, "*Trust me. He is my uncle, and he is a handsome man. Besides that, he gave us the authority to see and find a woman that he* can trust and sharpen his focus on the value of love, and that's why I came to see you. Because you are the only one fitted for the situation, nobody else, "My entire family is in favor of you, and they have all their eyes on you. We, all, voted for you because you are a very nice person, a best friend of mine, and we all know you. We like you very much. We never lose the courage to take our opportunity or the determination to win. The goal, though, is not to win, but to make good first impressions, raising the importance of the role of love, helping you both transition— slowly—from strangers to lovers..."

Anyway, she wrote her uncle back; and in the letter, she gave him my name. The end result: we started writing letters to each other, and he became my pen pal as my faraway friend.

Shortly after we became friends, he told me "Can you please send me your picture so we can see each other?"

I answered him back with "Send me your picture first, then I will send mine in the next letter."

I was so excited for his next letter, dreaming to see him in picture and thinking about how he looked and how I would feel. That, again, was only natural. I was just curious, especially since he's abroad. I also got to thinking if he was just as curious about me and what he thought about my being a Filipina; then, I decided that he was just as anxious to see my picture.

It didn't take long for him to finally send his picture, and immediately after, I sent mine. Since then, we got to know each other; and we started answering our letters as soon as we received them—it didn't matter what time of the day it was. The downside was we had to wait fifteen days for our letters to reach us. That's how it was during the '70s, before cell phones were available. I didn't even know how to use a computer! There was no such thing as e-mail during that time. There was a long-distance phone;

but I had to go to the city, in which was about ninety-eight kilometers from my hometown. And it was much too expensive to make a long-distance call anyway. So of course, we had to write letters to contact somebody abroad and just got used to it.

Needless to say, it was just a very hard time

With technology as poor as it was; there were simply no better means of communicating with our loved ones in faraway places. But despite all that, I had been able to grasp the key to one of the great doors in my love history.

I waited until Josh's letters became available even though our relationship remained the same, and I stayed blissful in our exchange until my very enticing love story left it up to us to decide whether or not we should try for something more than friendship. We chose to be pen pals in the beginning and started asking about each other's hobby, favorite song, favorite color, favorite food, relationship status, and etc. He was so cool, and I enjoyed writing back to him. He always finished his letters with "Your faraway friend, Josh."

Of course, that time I was hiding all these letters—though they were innocent and friendly enough—because of my parents (did I already mention that they were very strict?). They wanted a plain shortcut. "Studies first," they said. "No matter what you do, study first." And being the dutiful daughter that I was, I followed the rules. That was just the way to do things.

I somehow also convinced myself that I was obeying so that I can learn and study the rules of love.

Sometimes I didn't answer his letter because I was too busy for my studies. I didn't pay much attention anymore when I realized I could not be interested with him as someone more than a pen pal. At that time, my girlfriend said, Josh was forty-five years old; so he was a little too old for my liking. At this realization, I was reminded of the promise I made to myself. *I won't let my parents down and be disappointed with me while I am in school.*

I knew that love can wait, but not forever; I knew I'll be holding on from love until I lose my patience. Somehow my parents had found out about Josh. When they did, they said "Right now you have a pen pal abroad.

Make sure you study your subjects first in school and not your love letter from abroad."

"But love is just like a game. It can be played and won. You need to learn and know all the rules before you start to play the games. That's why despite of learning the love rules, you have to be able to spend your love life in your own—and nice—way."

What a beautiful, meaningful thought and advice! Remember, love is always in the air—like how there are always flowers, in all of the seasons.

I guess you have to understand that you'll never know just how much lonely life has been, but life began again the day you took my hand.

In the olden days, adults like the parents and (especially) the old school principal were of very strict cultures and beliefs. You just had to follow and understand their direction, especially when they tell you that love doesn't happen while you are studying in school. It has been the deep promises with you and them and to understand the language that your parents permitted you to do.

The conviction had been made: listen to your mind and not your heart and to your own intuitive wisdom when making important decisions, especially when deciding about a gift of destiny. Your mind and your heart know what you really need—either love or education.

But first I put it in my mind that it has to be a strong decision. First and foremost, I chose education the starting point of making permanent and lasting changes in my life, with my understanding of the difference between feeling in love with somebody first, or achieving my education before I decided to settle myself.

So, I'm just telling you not to follow your heart; follow your brains, and study first. I have no desire to see anyone else—at least, until I'm done with my education.

Despite warnings from my parents, I was too young. That I did not have enough experience to make such a critical love life decision also reinforced the value of my parents as an overall role maintained of their values. My parents' idea was if I ever have a boyfriend, I might have to stop going to school; and my hope of becoming a teacher would be dashed.

I wished that I had been more careful with all the things I had to do, and that I had the focus to remember. I found out if you listened to your parents' advice, you will not be lying down on the wet grasses in the future. Yes, it was very true; so I made myself pay attention to my parents saying "Since you are going to continue your studies, you have to make sure you'll never make mistakes. That's the promise."

I think my parents were right. I have put my love away when I was at school. I did not use it, thanks to their advice. When you are in love or when you love what you are doing, you don't notice that the time had just gone by the wind as it disappears; and you forget about it.

My dream of becoming a teacher never failed; this dream had come true because I've made a strong decision to do it. I finally did. I reached my goal successfully.

To the degree that I concentrate my efforts, I reached in and succeeded in what I want out of my love life desire. It was my desire to honor my parents, and they were my bosses in life.

Looking back into the mirror, I promised to be patient and disciplined because that was how to make myself a winner. I know when winners make mistakes: they'd say they were wrong. But when losers do, they'd say that it was not their fault. Everyone has values. I have values, but I have a virtue also to prove that truth is indispensable. That's the thing to be achieved in my love life: to be true to myself, and to live up to my potential so I can show my method and techniques being in love.

I love what I do, and I love my daily routine. My love lifestyle easily proved that the more success you earn in your job, the happier your love life (and the smoother everyone else's) can be. Love will be someone who acknowledges both the good and the bad in you yet loves you just the same—enthusiastically and successfully.

The secret of my success was to accomplish to the best of my capabilities what I have to do, and to think that I can do almost anything and everything. I did not forget about whether I might win or lose, and by doing so, I worked hard and practiced my skills that I really love. I wanted to set the records about my life.

I never entertained any lover that has come into my life before or any offer of a love story because I knew love can wait, if you are willing to pay the price.

Life is what the mind's love can conceive, and it can be achieved by believing in it. The problem is that some individuals do not set goals of their love life in the first place. I did not have much trouble achieving my own goals. But people have delighted themselves in love and have begun on a long journey that will be coming on the appointed day, and it has been said that the everlasting love goes on for a long period of time without speaking; but never question that one day will come the intruder of the beginning initiation of the enticing love life story.

That, to be sure, is too good to be true and a fantasized shining love abroad.

Love is a matter of habit in a dream; and you can develop successful habits in your mind every day. If you let that love live daily and think about it always in your mind, then it will become a problem. You have to learn how to use that love.

As I said before, if you happen to find love in your life, you have to make sure to use your brain first and not your heart. If there is a shortcut to falling in love, then do not waste time in reinventing the wheel! Examine the love lifestyle and behavior of someone you love, emulate the good, and reject the bad.

The way to make love true is to be maintained in the good bonding opinion and a good relationship with each other. Love is worth finding. If you have known me before you would understand my love. Obviously, do not admit love right away for the first time; but if you examine your love life properly, one day at a time, the one love you want to have eventually who does not really fall in love with you will just fade away.

I should know this because it was my experience before I was inspired by my boyfriend so many times. I hoped I inspired him. When asked, none of us truly knows how much our significant others love us. It's such a waste to spend any true love of who is that the present time is not the critical decision of love. Love turn out best, for their love makes the best and of the way love turns out most if you get too much. You will not see what happens to the enticing love story.

It begins from the heart then moves toward the mind and acquires love. But with your decision scale and favorable comments from your friends that your love life decision works, you have used your brain and not your heart. By maintaining your proper love life, you require strict adherence to your brain's thought of understanding.

Keep reminding yourself that you are not as easy to get, nor are you narrow or hard to follow directly from your heart. Rather, you have adopted a new, loving philosophy, a new kind of loving advice from your parents being positive and enthusiastic about your love life habits. You can change your way of loving.

This is similar to the Christians following the great commandment to "love the Lord your God with all your heart, with all your soul, with all your strength, and with all your mind" and to "love your neighbor as you love yourself." It is like finding a new religion, and you are merely following the:

Ten Commandments Of Love

"*As listed below:*"

- Be conscious of falling in love; use your brain and not your heart.
- Be careful; love right and fall in love light.
- Settle your love only when you are finished with your education.
- Love only when you are ready to get ahead with your best idea of a love life.
- The problem that keeps plaguing in your mind is to love the junk love.
- Follow your dreams so that they would come true.
- Improve yourself by doing a tremendous job.
- Let the words of love come from your heart and mind.
- Keep the expectation of "how soon can I get my enticing love life?" steady.
- Ask yourself "How do I know I'm getting the right love perish forever?"

Remind yourself that love is getting what you give, and happiness is the inspiration of your love.

Whoever therefore breaks one of the commandments listed above and tells people to do so shall be called least in the kingdom of heaven, but whoever does and teaches them to follow shall be called great in the kingdom of heaven.

According to Bobby McFerrin, "In every life, we have some trouble. When you worry, you make it double."

So do as the song says. *Don't worry and be happy! According to the teenagers, "Hang in there!" or "Hang loose!" Whatever will be, will be, if it is to be, let it be.* If there was more laughter, there would be happier people; and that's like they are looking for more lovers. If you want to change, hold on together. Love will contribute to the highest level of being in love.

Always be ready to whisper, and listen to your heart and mind. This inner portion of your love is ready to understand and to control the situation to remove the doubts about your relationships. Change the world with your loving acts of confidence. Prove by your life that love is real and lives through you. *Someone else will say "Forget it. I'll just find somebody else!"* But no matter who you will find or choose to be with, you will have to live with that certain person. You've got to commit yourself to a plan.

I thought I'd be stuck forever, and I cannot move anywhere else; but I have to be able to go forward and find a new beginning so I will not look back anymore from wherever I was stuck. I wanted to move on, to move forward because success in love does not just happen overnight. It truly proves that both lovers have to build a strong foundation and have to be willing to work hard to achieve that love.

I love her or him very much. I hoped you understand my love life. It isn't easy to explain but action speaks louder than words. The life of our love shall seek to be patient in our daily trials and shall look for ways to be of service in loving and understanding. A tender, loving caring is the flavor to win the enticing love from beginning to end.

I would say congratulations to you on stepping out of your comfort zone, in taking the first step toward a new, loving beginning in your love life. *Remember that there are three things that keep you from ever reaching on how to succeed in love:* fear to tell the truth, uncertainty to fall in love, and doubt to say "I do."

But those are not good enough reasons to say "There are more reasons to say 'I love you with all of my heart.'"

Don't hide in the darkness, and come out into the light.

That would be like to call fourth fight by becoming a loving sweetheart. By committing to fall in love with each other, both of you are kicking out your egos to find the new opportunity, and to work hard to help your love lives be a success which will serve as a hosting pad to a new lover and loving beginning.

Some of you would like to ask yourselves *"Why should I fall in love with this person? What's in it for her or him?"* I mean the reality is love at first sight is natural; it will not just happen overnight, so you've got to commit yourself to a game plan and be willing to understand that love situation to achieve that love success as much as it excess.

You must listen to my advice. I know because I've been there. It was my experience—each of the four men I mentioned proposed a different scheme for the same version history of love.

According to the old song *"Que Será Será"* by Jay Livingston and Ray Evans, "Whatever will be, will be. The future's not ours to see . . ." But we keep thinking that we can just wish and that our luck will make our wishes come true. Most people can see their future picture to plan in him or her. *Yes, you can.*

There is a good future which was currently running in every prestige of the everlasting love if you focus such law of love a faithful opinions, as well. Hitch a ride to be with your love if you are willing to agree with that love.

To achieve that love affair into a big success of your love life, simply don't give up too early. You know, most sweethearts put up their hardest love at first time they meet; and if they don't get along immediately, they split up. These are the same people that would jump to find a new boyfriend or girlfriend, and that is not a good idea.

I have found out that love is so much more than a common thing for everybody. They say that falling in love is wonderful, and it is very true.

Each waking moment of our love life has a special place in our hearts, and the thoughts make you wander without conscious direction; but only you can make a decision. Everybody has different ideas of a true desire of the inspirational feeling of love.

Kept that loved in our own special way. Who do you want to be with? Somebody to enjoy a feeling of deep satisfaction and comfort in your own thoughts and doubts? In such a case, you will not feel that you have lost your love. Let the spirit of love be your guide that made your love stay stronger forever.

Through all those years, you both felt the same in love; but neither one of you knew how little you are in giving a portion of love. If you have a relationship script similar to this, then it is the time for you to shift the turning point of your love. If you discovered that the vast majority of your love life's problems grew—especially problems wherein you were jealous of somebody else—then solve that problem right away unless you are willing to accept it.

On the contrary of love and understanding, it's really up to you to move into a new beginning; and if he or she has a good reason to explain, then just gave him or her a second chance so that they can receive the approval in the benefit of the doubt. And just don't do the same thing all over again. Start by loving again and again, and be careful with the promises because promises are not made to be broken.

Broken is not a good thing and will leave you terribly brokenhearted in a relationship with a terrible love life story. Maybe it is meant to be. Perhaps it is what it is, from the beginning to end.

Just like the Holy Bible saying in Proverbs 26:27–28, "Whoever digs a pit will fall into it, and he who rolls a stone will have it roll back on him. A lying tongue hates those who are crushed by it, and a flattering mouth works ruin."

Something would come to my mind. There was an act of virtue beyond imagination, a promise that "our love will be forever, until the end of our life. And my love will not change till the end of my last breath." You are unaware or might be forgetting those promises, and suddenly your relationships create a very big problem and will end up on that moment.

Never underestimate the power of love that you release on this planet. *Imagine if today were the last day of our love, and you see the defining moments ending up now, what will you say? You cannot say "We will do it all over again." Do you think your intended statements really work?* Perhaps you are one of those lovers who think that it is a good idea to approach that person after he or she has walked away. Your heart will never fail, and you will never be falling in love and will be sorry. Know your own love life's worth.

It had been my experience. I was almost always sure to rub somebody I know and love the wrong way when I make a stand for who I really love.

But on that moment, I have the good reason to believe on my own beliefs.

I knew I already had Dr. Bob and Josh from Hawaii. But that was not a good enough reason to stop.

I still had more reasons to continue to find a message of loving kindness and worth of love. *Things that I would really swear! "Damn!" What should I do?" And my mind clicked. What was it?*

I knew I had a handful of choices: Bob, Josh, Fred, and Lloyd. All of them have carried their ability and professionalism of choice. I was searching for the answers. My family always told me "Which once are you prepared to dominate your love life?

"The dollar or the peso?"

I hoped that the path I had chosen has always been the right one I thought.

Where do I begin? It's too hard to tell the story of the love. I just can be . . . I am not. Totally nothing very special in me but, of this, I am sure.

But my love and dedication and hard work were the art of natural living in a passionate way.

A Significant Affair
to Remember

It was early November 1974, and I was assigned to teach at Tanjay College in Tanjay, Negros Oriental. I met Mr. Fred at a party. Mr. Fred was a school teacher at Tanjay Elementary School. His favorite quotes were:

"When I fall in love, it will be forever" (Nat King Cole, "When I Fall in Love"); and "The winners in life think constantly in terms of I can, I will, and I am" (Denis Waitley).

He stepped onto the floor and began to approach me, walking easily. He suddenly stopped right where I was sitting down on a chair. He then sat next to me and introduced himself. He said, "One of the things I love the best is to sit down with you and share stories." He then asked if he could dance with me. I said yes, and we started dancing with each other while sharing stories and asking questions.

We were laughing and were just joyful throughout that evening. He did not dance with anybody but me, and I knew that meant he has feelings for me. We danced through all the songs and barely even noticed the last song was over. He told me that the music was not important to him as long as he can dance with me. "Do not be afraid to take a chance," he said.

"Remember, the greatest failure is to not try."

Once you have something you love to do, according to his principle, there is no royal flower-strewn path to success. He said that if there is, he has not found it yet and that if there is, he has accomplished everything in his love life. It is because he had been willing to work hard. *As Napoleon*

Hill best put it in his book (co-authored with Dennis Kimbro) Think and Grow Rich: A Black Choice, "Whatever the mind can conceive and believe, it can achieve." Apply your heart to instruction of love wisely, and guide your love in the way your heart will hear your burning desire.

Mr. Fred said, "I couldn't believe why I feel this way in the dance show format, for this is the perfect choice of my love life. You are my love, the power of my life. The most challenging time is now. I told my friendly star how wonderful you are.

It is true! I can see that in you.

That's why I'm so in love with you."

I replied, "Are you kidding me?

It is too soon to be believed! I do not know you that much. Plus, this is the first time we met!"

For a long time, all he could do was stare at me, without moving his eyes. But in my part, it was only a big joke in my innermost being. I was only speaking of the right thing. My heart instructed me to become impatient to be free.

The dancing event on that night was faster on both of us. He asked me "What do you want in your life?" I answered, "I hope and I pray that my dreams for the future will all come true." At that moment, he watched me so closely though it really didn't matter to me. All I could think about was how I could afford to accept his special love for me. Slowly in the back of my head, I looked back to Dr. Bob and Josh's picture.

Mr. Fred interrupted my train of thought. "Oh my goodness! 'Unless otherwise agreed to in writing, any agreement may be subject to change.

If it will not work, goods must be returned. Please keep your receipt.'" Awkward silence followed.

Shortly after, he finally said *"Just joking! You're entitled to rely and are solely responsible for your love."*

I was working on my lesson plan for next week, and Mr. Fred came suddenly. He felt guilty about showing up without warning. He hadn't said anything, an object without feeling, of the subject, what and where and how he thought of me today. I had thought that it would be easier somehow, that I would tell him my feelings for him; but I also didn't say anything.

Everything that came into my head seemed inappropriate, and so I kept my mouth quiet and control my thoughts.

Mr. Fred continued communicating with me, and sometimes he visited me at my boarding house. I did not know and could not answer why it was so important for him to come over when it's not time or not the weekend yet. To this, he replied *"This visit from me is for you. Today is special. That makes all my love worthwhile for me."* He stared at me for long time and held his hands by the door that inspired me nothing. I looked at him with a stern expression. He looked back to me and weakened his face. I gave him a signal that hopefully he took as me saying *"Do not come in the school!"* After that, he realized I truly didn't want him visiting me at the school.

I put him aside and remembered Josh always sending me a letter from Hawaii. He said in his letter once *"I want to go to the Philippines and I want to marry the lady you know."* But I didn't pay attention because it was just a dream for me. We were not talking about love yet; I did not put too much any weight on it. We corresponding letters all the way, and his closing remarks always said *"Your faraway friend."* There was no more *"love"* at the end. And so I was just hanging loose. But I think he learned some things as well. I answered his letter, saying *"I have somebody else over here so you better stop sending any letters for me already."*

In 1974, Josh vacationed in the Philippines for a month. There we met each other. He decided to come and visit me in the Philippines (the first time in his life to see the country). So when he had just arrived from his flight, he was asking where my house was; and he said he was pleased because his nephew had come forward to accompany him to come to my house.

When he got there, we shook hands with each other and talked.

He said, "You are a hardworking lady."

I said, "Thank you."

He dropped his voice until it was just a little bit audible.

He said, "I miss you, and I love you so much."

I said, "At last! Seeing each other is the best."

He was silent for a moment as he reached for my hands and kissed them. He then bowed his head and wondered what was coming next. His two deep-brown eyes flickered very impatiently. It seemed he liked me very much I could tell by the way he acted. I coughed and, through squinted eyes saw his mouth whispering to me *"I love you."* I didn't answer him.

Josh was a simple, plain man. He always wore jeans. He looked like James Bond in a way; he was not handsome but had the look that made you like him. He was a nice, humble, and smart person. He worked at McBryde Sugar Company as a mill machine operator, He loved his job and worked over there for forty-eight years then retired. He has a tendency to think others were smarter or wiser than we are. Josh was also a good guitar player. He played and sang songs to me, and I sang songs to him too.

He sat down on the chair and looked at me steadily. We talked about how we felt about each other from our previous pen pal letter acquaintances.

We were very happy, going over them again and again. After so many months of correspondences, he wondered what was coming next; and he decided to propose marriage and felt good that he would accomplish most of what he wanted to do. I had always come to believe that it was the time for me to come clean about all my other suitors. My intended statement must conform to the secrecy of my belief, so I held back at that time and didn't decide yet.

A year after that, I was assigned to teach in another part of Cebu. My answer was either yes or no. I decided I would go. I think everyone has their own set of mind. I have been acquainted with Mr. Fred for a year. And so when I told him about it, I said, quoting Aerosmith, "I have to move, and sorry to say, 'I'm leaving on a jet plane."

Mr. Fred replied, quoting a poem by an unknown author, "'Love is not how you forget, but how you forgive. Not how you listen, but how you understand. Not what you see, but of how feel. And not how you let go, but how you hold on.' I will hold on to it because I love you very much, heart to heart."

I am so very happy I put my trust to myself and God. Through Him, all things are possible. Thank you, Father God, for never forgetting or leaving me, for being my savior, for always loving me unconditionally. I owe you my life, and that's why I pray to you always; and my faith is in my heart. You said "Follow your heart and you will find your mind." Also, "Follow me, and I will show you the way. I will have someone to take care of you, and that's me." Thank you, Father God, for giving me the knowledge to know where I am going.

I went ahead and moved to where I was assigned to teach, Madridejos National High School. Of course, you would feel sad for the first time you spend your days in a different place, especially if you don't know anybody.

I thought to myself, Now it's time to recharge and get some motivation for myself with this powerful investment of my life. I guess that's how it is if you are a new teacher or are new in a job—they will transfer you to different places.

Anyway, I was so happy too after all. The school inspired me all students of mind. They boosted their sprit and rekindle the passion that first inspired me to become a good teacher. But I never really found out what I believed in until I began to instruct and to teach my students. It takes a special person to be a teacher: it has to be someone patient, kind, and enthusiastic.

The first step I had to reprogramming a limited study is to become aware of the subject that you are going to teach and if you are holding it.

For the next couple of days, I had good news about opening themselves to the truth reflected. Ultimately, I had seen the students that had power and love in the subject. When I see something like, I know I am doing a good job. Thanks be to God! It was the answer to my prayers. I have to continue my belief, my action, and my attitude.

I've found that luck is quite predictable. If you want more luck, take more chances. You know it's true. It did not take too long. There was an invitation for all the teachers to attend the town fiesta at Madridejos. It was presented and sponsored by the principal of the school. All teachers must attend, and to my surprise, I had a very special invitation. They told me that I had to go as well. I didn't feel much like going, and when the teachers were ready, my energy was conspicuously low.

On the same time, there was a gentleman who came to me and introduced himself as Mr. Lloyd, with a smile. He turned around to face me and said "Ms. Silvano, I don't know you, but I've heard lately that you just transferred to teach in this school. So would you please join all the teachers attending the town festival? For so long, I have known it is fun if everybody comes." That changed my dynamic performance. To be a professional, it was certainly acknowledged. He said, "No one will be impressed by our words if we are not present in the festival." I listened to him, and I noticed he smiled too.

He was an electronic engineer. He told me *"I just came back from the city to attend this event, and I was so inspired to hear that there is a new teacher transfer from another island. And so I came to see you."* We were sitting in front of the stage with the nice music, and we were dancing together. I knew he was interested in me, and his reaction proved that to me as well. There is something much more special. Now what? I knew and understood then why my choice was so hard.

It is very important that each partner have a basic understanding of their relationship. The key of love is to receive the riches of the happiness that lies in our willingness to accept the good partnerships. God can give us all the blessings in our life, but if we are not willing to accept them, they go unwanted; and disaster is predicted. We live in the beautiful world of an ocean of good. It is up to us to let our love adore the everlasting reign with sweet, loving partnerships of our choice.

Looking back, I found it hard to choose. Dr. Bob is still in my heart, thinking back. He is always there when I go home (he is my neighbor).

The life of our love shall seek to be patient in our daily trials, and shall look for ways to be of service in loving for a new beginning. This love of mind, these inner fainthearted can be applied to anybody's limiting words and other phrases of loving kindness. *"Love is a many- splendored thing."*

Yes, that is very true.

There are fundamental laws of love to which all other laws conform. The law of cause and effect means the results of these love situations must be equal to the cause of ideas and belief. The action and reaction of two people together is just a dream—like the old folks saying *"Love is blind but lovers cannot see,"* meaning they don't know if they are compatible.

As long as they fall in love together, they don't really know their character.

Until they come a long, their hearts wait just for the two of them, thinking of their future and forever and their loving care. I know this because I have been there; it was my experience, and it is my duty to help you to learn the life of love.

What you still need to do about love is to master the gift of life; and that's the tender, loving care. Imagine a time before you were born. Your mother loved you from where you were, inside of her womb. It may be that the love will look on her as an affliction, and that you will repay her with good, loving care to the best of your ability when you grow up. That love is an endless love. If you could allow that to happen when you find a love of your own, then start to turn your love lifestyle when you're ready to turn a small key, which ignites the engine in your heart and mind.

Now I have warned you to use your brains and not your heart when you choose a love relationship. It is much more important to review and to have a good look at your relationships with your action, reaction, and the respect for each other than anything else. If you want to be created in your love lifestyle, it's up to you. You will know who your love is meant to be with. If you want to be with him or her forever, you must know the feeling.

I know both lovers' minds say

You are my hope and my dream.
I hope you will be mine."
What can a love has to be spoken to say "I love you"?

It is essentially intended to love and to treat it with total respect that receives the power or energy from the bottom of everybody's heart that are involved in love.

Have you ever heard the song
"It's a Sin to Tell a Lie"
by Billy Mayhew? It goes "Millions of hearts have been broken just because these words were spoken. I love you. Yes, I do."

The universe is like a river that keeps on flowing, the river doesn't care who will use—whether happy or sad, rich or poor, good or bad, handsome or beautiful, and young or old. The waters just keep on flowing nobody can stop the river because that is natural. It is such a lucky river's flowing going over to reach the beautiful blue ocean of good. Some lovers go down to visit the river and they cry, some lovers go down to visit the river and play they can jumped in and down and they are happy, but the river's does not care it just keeps flowing because it is impersonal. The world cannot stop turning, and the sun cannot stop burning, because they are impersonal.

A question is asked

Why does the sun keep on shining?

I am not sure for the answer; I'm still searching for it. I've found that mattered which have come true. In this life, I was loved by you. Love can be a joyful, peaceful experience in our daily walks of life. *Our actions can be guided by our loving sweetheart's support. In creativity and unique understanding of our love relationships, what was the direct source of understanding? By loving forevermore, was it the love connection? No, it wasn't. It was tender, loving care (TLC).* A dependent source of everyone's life, it has to be charged up and mastered to a higher level of love. I paused for just a moment and remembered all the things that happened.

Kindness is best insurance of happiness

Sometimes we are frightened to be all that we can be because of the wrong choices we make; it upsets other people involved. Well, since we don't want to hurt ourselves, we must think first before we do it—as a way to get ourselves to continue to do what our minds decided, and our hearts will just follow the flow.

How could you do that? How could you hurt me that way? Some comments may say, I can't make it without you. You are the source of my happiness. In reality, you don't hold someone else's happiness in your heart; and no one holds your happiness in their hearts either. When you are alone, your love life runs the risk of rejection; and the more you fear rejection, the more you seek for approval. Find every opportunity to break the hard ice; then, you will be free. You'll never know what made your love run away, how can you keep searching when dark clouds hide the day.

After a couple of years, things turned out good for me. I was constantly just becoming used to my daily routine in the school. Nothing in this wide world left for me to see, but I keep on waiting till you return. I totally forgot about my secret love from abroad. I did not answer his love letters. It appeared that I didn't want to be bothered with entertainment. Every second that passed, as I made my way from my boarding house onto the edge door of the school, was burned into my mind forever and the other enticing love stories of my love life.

The most important thing of my life was to challenge every good about love life because I was not afraid to take advantage or take any chances in love, and I was just practically busy all the time at work. But I kept on waiting until the days I learned that heavy, dark clouds that came with the wind and without rain were terrifying.

It was the scariest moment of my life; then, I was very surprised because my lover, Josh, arrived from Hawaii. He vacation in the Philippines for one month. Evening came, and the only dream that mattered had come through. It was the turning point of my life. Little did I know that the day would be the starting point of my love life.

Obviously, the greatest failure of being in love was to not try to fight the right of being a strong woman. If you try to forget the enticing love story in your life, it will come soon constantly in terms *of I can, I will, and I am.*

In other words, an individual lover's love from abroad; and there are three individuals that their love involved in our relationships were better, and they pretended it's true and it wasn't easy to do.

Those lovers pick up their phones like they just spoke yesterday. Regardless of how long it has been, or how far away they live, they don't hold grudges. They understood that the world was mine and can't be theirs (my friends'), *so why should they pretend?* If you're happy-go- lucky, so your lives are busy. *But beside that, luck is what happens when I intend the harder I work, the luckier I get.* I've always loved myself and my love lifestyle. *Yesterday was history, then tomorrow is a mystery, and today is a gift. That's why they called it a present—or now and forever.*

Those lovers should know who they are. They both were handsome and had their own values in their love lives, motives, and their complete acceptance. Bob, Fred, Josh, and Lloyd left long-lasting good impressions.

They followed their dreams, and they were not afraid to go back and stand under that one red flower and walk straight ahead to their own destination.

Whatever the minds of the individuals can conceive and believe, it can achieve love, thoughts, and powerful things when mixed with definiteness of love, and burning desire.

The determination of love, that whether you are loved or not being loved, you completely did your jobs the best way indeed, make sure to do the best you can every day. Be a positive thinker every moment.

Adopt and use the right thinking so that you can enjoy the promises of your love life style. Decide to tell your lovers "*We have the ability to fall in love right now, but we need to know the rules of love and understand our love affair. This can wait until we sure have done our education.*"

Happy, successful, motivated people dare big dreams. If you are, then you know our love life gradually expands into a satisfyingly full condition; and you care more than love as an excellent love. If you are really in love with somebody, you will never find other love in anybody. But you must understand these very important facts. Maybe you are just kidding to your love life or to yourself.

A simple advice for lovers: do not admit the love offer in one affair. You must take and make time for it and find time to evaluate and to really, really understand it. Whoever wastes time to find it has not discovered the value of love life. Absolutely great things have no fear of time and love. Do not agree to any offer. Think first of what is good, before you say yes. Follow your dreams. Do not follow your heart, but follow your mind and think and evaluate first what is good.

Secret Love

Once I had a secret love, I concentrated my walking love life on what I should have or would have done, or what I can't do it to follow my dreams had come true. Love will work according to your feeling and principle of physical law. If it does not work that way, then you could not keep the love affair functioning appropriately. Each of us has the ability to handle and manage the feelings of love. It is the game of life with balance, harmony, and joy; but I need to know the rules and the principles of love. There was no royal, red-and- white flower–strewn path to success; but if there was a possibility, there would be no such thing as gray or blue. I have not discovered it yet, and I had become well-to-do from doing what I do in anything in my love lifestyle. I was solely responsible for my enticing love story.

Josh said in his letter that he wrote this song especially for me. This song was dedicated to me personally, so we both knew what he meant. He said, "This is my inspiration and opportunity to sing to you, even if you are not around me at this moment in time." Opportunity can be spelled with four letters, but those letters are not *luck*; rather, they are *love*. If you have no purpose of love, you have no opportunity of being in love; and you sold yourself out. When the mindless, unchallenging routine existence and safety are blending accepted and become unthinking goals. So trust yourself. Allow the enticing love story the information of your heart and mind that enables you to go out and create the love without stress, and without effort to come through.

What happened to this fascinating love life story of mine? What is it all about? I'm sure I haven't done in trouble, but if I did, I need a helping hand of learning how the relationships should work, might work, and do not work. I tried to fill my love and closed my eyes and thought of you.

I always remember all winter-long reading Josh's couple of love letters said *"I love you very much."* I became what I chose to become: a lover's love.

Obviously, man has the unique gift of love, has the ability to reason. Beings use logical ideas to hold you and to become what they think about controlling the thoughts. Actually, I am who I am that created my unique form of identity habits and comfort zones. Keeping of what I was thinking was all up to me. No matter what route I take, I share the awesome journey of the enticing love life story to the mountaintop of reaching my destination of love, and to claim the beauty of the enticing love life story. I have so much to talk about! *Letters become word, words become sentences, and sentences become paragraphs.*

As I tried to read Josh's letters, I didn't want to steal his thunder. "It is a continual adventure," he said. "I live loving you. I love you so much that it almost hurt my mind, thinking and dreaming of you." He thought for the most part that he had been happier was the time since he started writing to me as his pen pal. But I knew I had a fighting chance for all my lovers.

I have come to realize that there was a way to get beyond the fear. I was afraid the situation will become a fighting point about all of my hiding love like *Josh, Dr. Bob, Fred, and Lloyd.* I looked at the situation, thought of myself and the trials of love. One thing that was most destructive to my feeling good was my self-inflicted guilt. Why had they picked me? I did not pick them. Believe it or not, *I'm not pretty or beautiful; but I know I looked beautiful to the man who loved me before.* I wondered whether my love life attracts them such that they believe me to be truly beautiful. If I am using imagery to change habit patterns to entertain these fellows, I often seem to have a different and new lover's love. A fascinating love story that has no stops from the beginning and no ending about my enticing love life.

I have many fond memories that provide no known benefit and cannot change my secret love story; what will happen tomorrow between *Dr. Bob, Fred, Josh, and Lloyd*; the confusion greatly affected my peace of mind and left me powerless. The connection between the love and the result, makes quality memories and became an inspiration. Thus, choosing a theme song that goes with your feelings was easier.

Josh sent me a letter and wrote a song to me as our theme song. He said "and I love you so," No matter what, Ultimately, Josh was able to totally rethink, pushed his mind wrote a letter to his relatives in the Philippines and told them he's coming for a vacation someday. Josh finally did, and he was happy he did.

He felt that he's like on top of the world, and he thanked *God* for that fountain of water springing up into everlasting love. Josh was wondering if he was destined to be alone forever, thinking he has to go back to Hawaii by himself again, something he wasn't sure he wanted and he has never tried.

The moment right before he arrived in the Philippines, there was something in his mind that needed to be resolved. His intention was to go home to Hawaii with his new wife. He wanted to settle in marriage right here at this very moment while he was in the Philippines. He was thinking he was forty-eight years old now; he's too old to be lonely. He hadn't dated anybody since he'd become a bachelor and promised to change his life forever.

His father died when he was fifteen years old. He was concerned about his mother and there were two of them in the family. He has one sister who was already married, and his mother died five years after his father passed away. He managed to live alone working every day at McBryde Sugar Company as a machine operator. His dedication and love for his work was amazing; the most loving inspiration one could ever ask for. He's thankful that for my love.

"Oh, yes! It's hot!"

There was not a breath of air in Badian, Cebu, Philippines, and the block of coconut trees as it gave shade to the afternoon heat. My girlfriend visited me to tell the story of Josh's personal experience in life. She wanted to convince me about him. Remember, you cannot change your thinking of what you do not acknowledge. The only thing in the world you can change is yourself and that makes all the difference in the world. We talked of old stories of love in our place with a smile.

Obviously, it made me realize that it makes a lot of sense. I've always wondered why, how this love can do to you and dream up exotic ways: I though it's a great set up, amazing. What puzzled me all those days was I have already a boyfriend—Dr. Bob. We just kept cool in our relationship, a secret because our parents were so strict at that time. You know old folks; they follow their forefathers' behaviors.

They don't want to see their teenagers being kissed until they get married. They have their rules in place. If ever I find a boyfriend or get into any relationship, then I have to stop schooling. What's funny because Dr. Bob was my neighbor we lived in the same town, so we just pretend our relationship does not exist, not even in a romantic way.

Our relationship acts like according to the greatness of excellent love: if love is for us, who can be against our love? During that time, I was a second year college student at Southwest Coast College in Badian, and Dr. Bob's mom was one of my instructors at the college. His mom likes me very much as a student in that school.

I was one of the honor students in our class. There was one event in the college when they had to choose the campus queen, *Miss Southwest Coast College Queen* of the year, and I was lucky I was chosen to become one. I became the queen. That was the best and most memorable moment in my life: to become a queen in our college. My parents, family, friends, and relatives were very proud of me and I was very happy too.

There were many activities held during that time, and Dr. Bob's mom always consulted me if I could be in charge or if I could be a leader on such activities. There were times when dancing activities were held together with the entire college students and teachers and we did. For some reasons, you have to choose your own personal partner. And all of a sudden Dr. Bob's mom chose me to be her partner. When dancing at the College, I felt shy because they were the owner of the school, and they are a very rich family.

Dr. Bob's father is a doctor too and his mom is the dean of the college. And I was thinking, why, I was wondering, maybe he told his mom about our relationships because she was close to me? And you know, he is the one and only son of his parents. During that year, Dr. Bob was living in the city to continue his career. We didn't have any communication or did not see each other because we were far apart.

In the following year, I have to transfer to the city to continue my studies, at Southwestern University, the sister school in the city, because Southwest Coast College did not offer the subjects in order for me to finish my college course, bachelor of science in education. So all subjects were credited to that school I have a dream to become a teacher, so I continued my studies because I want to become somebody. I want to embark on a journey of education that could profoundly change my life, and offer my own mind a practical way to create anything I love or desire.

Success is a result, not a goal, and also I wanted to grab the opportunities to use my talent and to be a successful person. If you believed in your love, don't ever give up.

Overall, I handled my love relationship with Dr. Bob very much appropriately. Everything was based on proven love techniques and timeless principles on love while with Dr. Bob. Shortly before I graduated from college, He visited me one weekend at my boarding place, together with his friend. One of them was also a boyfriend of my other girlfriend living together with me in our boarding house.

We just talked about his love for me never fading; he was a wonderful man. I thought he was the type that I would want to share my life with. He was also kind and gentle. I enjoyed his visits. He was a student doctor at that time; and almost done with his studies.

He knew that I have a friend named Josh from abroad but I told him, no big deal he's just a faraway friend of mine. And then sometimes it is just easier not to think about it and it was okay for him. I was so happy and comfortable about everything.

My relationship with Dr. Bob was so peaceful. But I remembered him and he remembered me. Things turn out best for us he made himself available and I am also available.

It was not so long ago we met and our meeting wasn't adjourn yet, we have to discuss our new business and talk stories to learn our own thoughts if we can become a reality if we believe those thoughts to be true.

Despite our love relationships, we recognized our own beings as the only assurance to tell the time, and the greatest way to get to know our feelings. We cannot earn happiness by doing something that makes us unhappy. You cannot get bananas from the coconut tree, and you cannot climb the coconut tree if you don't have a ladder. The ladder doesn't care whoever climbs it, as long as one holds on to it.

Loving is the key to success in your love relationship. Love is a game; it can be played and won just like football; we need to learn and study it and know all the rules. *If you want to spend your entire lifetime in the games then you should learn and play to win.*

Success in love is the big road toward joy, and happiness is the reward for all your struggles. It is the result of loving what we truly believe. In order to achieve success in love, you have to figure out steps, think of ways to ease each other's burdens, and treat each day as a gift.

Ultimately, I was able to totally reengineer those parts of my love life, and to make the right decisions on those love that I felt who I will choose because I wanted to know what love is.

Love is not a gadget, love is not game, love is not a toy, but love dissolves fear and our love will gently grow. But I kept my love with Dr. Bob dealing between truth sincerity and integrity of the utmost importance to the reality of our love life, if that love was not ready yet to go, then I care very much about what I think of what I do.

Perhaps we were seeking for the answers to all our questions, answers that tell us who I really love the most. But I made sure to think before I say *"I do,"* I have to remember, think first, I used my mind and I did not use my heart.

Sometimes I receive the answers, but most of the time I don't receive it. I keep on seeking that answer. But he and I have the rest of our life to say, can anybody else feel the same the way we do? We knew our love was meant to be; it would never end till the end of our life.

I think it's very true, it is only our thoughts of love, attitudes, and emotions in the moment, when you are in love. Notice the power of love and desire, yearn and pray for that which is closest to your heart and mind. Nothing ever happened in the past and nothing will happen now.

That's right, but the question was, we did not continue to follow up the real right answer. Dr. Bob was very busy, only to find that within a few months or a few years, we were right back to where we were before! I just left it that way.

I was so occupied with my thoughts and was busy with my studies. I watched smilingly as I recall those memories. I glanced at Josh's love letters; my eyes were following my brains. I graduated with a degree in Bachelor of Science in Education.

October 1973 and must take the test to pass the board exam right away. Thank God I passed the test and the result was released on December 1973. The district office hired me to teach right away on January 9, 1974, at Tanjay College, Tanjay Negros Oriental.

I was just so lucky indeed I thought of each day I must work now I don't wait for tomorrow because tomorrow is another day. I seek this every minute of whatever I do.

Power & Magic of Love

This is my dream and I asked God to please give me the strength to fulfill my promise, the power and magic in it. So I proceeded to go to Tanjay College right on that moment. I kept myself busy with school work and school activities. As time goes by, time will reveal everything. If I have to work hard as time goes by fast and speaks even when not asked. It was not the time I put in that counts, it is what I put into my work because I really love what I do.

I am busy with school, when you do what you love, the payback is very rewarding; it's better to always nurture your outcome if you just know what to do with it. I can tell you about this, but nothing will be as convincing as your own exhausting results.

The summer right after I passed the board examination, I was assigned to work at Tanjay College, Tanjay Negros Oriental, Philippines, and the other island next to Cebu. I was surprised, worried, happy, and afraid I don't know what to do. Thinking, I don't know anybody in the island, and I have to start to find the place where I'm going to live, soon to start the classes.

It was such lovely and a lucky feeling my *brother Nick* helped me and came to the place where I taught. It was an opportunity for me knowing my *brother's army troop assigned at Barrack Tanjay* that time. He came to visit me to see how I was doing. Also I was glad my nephew *Rey,* he had just arrive from Badian, to apply a job to work at the school during the middle of the semester. So, he got the job. I was fully happy and secured; I enjoyed my job. I never worry about the two days in the week one is yesterday, and the other is tomorrow.

I taught algebra in the second year high school students and also first year college in mathematic. I was so busy every time, in fact, I forgot all the love activities as I don't have even time to read Josh's letter from abroad.

I can't afford my job to tearing it down making two lesson plans for college and high school. Besides, I enjoyed my job being a new teacher. I want to take the opportunity and have an experience to be a teacher. I found the concepts and ideas that may change the way you approach life in general.

Result of service is the outcome to succeed in your working career. Your rewards in life will earn you confidence and direct professionalism. I enjoyed my life teaching my students, I love them. They have become used to the way I handled the classes.

As time went by, I met someone far across the distance and space between us. Another Saturday night, it was a pleasant night but which grew increasingly tense. There was an invitation to all the teachers in our school to attend the fiesta event in the beautiful community. The occasion was for a party dance that was famous in *Tanjay, Negros Oriental*. I could remember we were dancing together and introduced his name.

"Hi, my name is Fred,
I'm a teacher at Tanjay Elementary School."

And so I took a deeper look and shook his nice strong hand. My eyes were opened wide and by the way, I made it through the night. We talked stories and probably Fred was getting a pretty good idea of just how important one's personality is in determining who one truly is.

Fred danced with me the whole time. It was he who taught me how to dance waltz, tango, chat cha, rumba, and we danced together until the music ended for the night.

I couldn't even dance with another man because he was always at my side. I was confused of what I think about love or what? It's now or never. I am amazed by the short-sightedness of most people to love and to be loved or to love at first sight.

As soon as everyone was ready to go home, I stood aside just to gaze at him. Fred seemed quite unaware of me. But he never knew at that time. I was observing him and that was only natural. In fact, I was thinking: what will happen to my faraway friend abroad and also with Dr. Bob?

But I don't know. I don't have any definite lover yet. I felt that I was in the same situation of being unnoticed as far as I'm concerned. I was thoroughly used to that, but afterward, I was so busy at school. I seemed not to care anymore even if there were some people who invited me to attend activities. *"I declined it."*

The standard method in those days for men declaring passion was that they usually try to use somebody to become a middle man, like a bridge or a go-between. One of my student related to him, approached me said, *"Miss Silvano, Mr. Fred wanted to visit you over here, and he said it is very important and maybe you know what it is."*

Weekend came and that was Saturday afternoon at 3:00 p.m. Mr. Fred came to our school cafeteria looking for me. One of the workers came to my boarding place and told me that I have a visitor waiting for me at the cafeteria, *"and that you should come right away."* So I went for sure. He was Mr. Fred; he was so happy to see me, an exciting love life, and maybe he also thought that this will lead somehow to a fruitful relationship. I looked at him, he was very handsome. So we talked stories. Then he said, *"I am a common man with common thoughts, and I've led a common life."*

That moment he offered his wonderful thoughts of love, and that he cannot find anybody else but me. "Would you please accept my offer?" Mr. Fred said, "I have something to tell you, my parents really wanted that I marry you anytime any day and they will provide as much as anything needed to express our marriage."

Now, remember they are very rich as they're part owner of the sugar company in Negros Oriental. It's a good feeling—the whole class of mine was aware and was watching what was going on.

The exciting process is like drilling for oil; you never quite know where the oil is; but the deeper you go, the better is your chance of striking in. Frequently, in the beginning, there was excitement. It was a pleasure to entertain Mr. Fred at the party. He doesn't want the evening to end, now that I'm around him. I'm not afraid of what he had to say, because in my heart, I already knew what it is all about.

As far as I'm concerned, I believed that I am not that pretty. I could hardly believe that the most handsome bachelors would notice me. Nothing can prevent and nothing can destroy love, I don't know who I will be choosing. I made a heartfelt promise to myself, that I will choose someone who loves me as I am, and treat me as if I'm the most beautiful woman in the world that knows the true value of love; and do more than strength, and take time to enjoy the present.

The Enticing Love Story

What happened to the enticing love story of mine and what is it all *about? Confused!* As the classes came to an end, and I am ready to go home where I lived at Badian, Cebu, Mr. Fred was lonely it's like one step forward and two steps backward, thinking I might just disappear.

It's never enough to say I love you, and not enough to say I care. But I'm caught between Mr. Fred and those three hidden lovers of mine wanting to get married to me. Lo and behold, I received a big brown envelope from the district office in Cebu stating that I will be transferred next year to teach at Madredejos Bantayan Island, Cebu. Before I went home, I told Mr. Fred, *"I want to tell you,* let's just be glad we had some time to talk, and make believe you loved me for the good times. I'll get along without you, if you'll find another love, and I'll be here for you if you should find you ever need me."

Unfortunately, Mr. Fred said, "Don't leave me now, now and forever my love is waiting for you, don't leave me now, don't say a word about tomorrow or forever, there'll be time enough for sadness when you leave me." "But I have to go home to Cebu." I cannot cry because I know that's weakness in his eyes, and I'm forced to fake a smile, a laugh. Every day in my love life I think we have very passionate relationships. Mr. Fred said, *"You are the only love of my life."*

I'm sorry I'm still trying to figure it out, what happened to my enticing love story? *And what is it all about?* To me, I will make you to see, all the things that your loving heart needs to know. I said, "I'm sorry I'm not available," which is true. And maybe he can stop loving me and I can't give him the approval of his love life offered to me.

Mr. Fred answered,

"To see is to believe."

Summer Love

Middle of summer 1975, Mr. Fred came to visit me in Badian where I lived. Unfortunately, I wasn't home. I went to the city to follow up on my papers for my next year's classes in the new school where I was going to transfer to teach. While he was coming down from the bus already after arriving in Badian, Mr. Fred met somebody in the road, and that somebody was my godmother. She was also a teacher at Badian Elementary School.

Mr. Fred approached her and asked information on where was Miss Silvano's house. He introduced himself, *"I am Mr. Fred, her friend from Tanjay, Negros Oriental. I want to visit and see her."* My godmother invited him to come inside my godmother's house since her house was just right there by the corner. She does not want to acknowledge his reasons at that moment. She wanted to know what his visit all about in Badian.

And finally, he confessed to my godmother that he loves me and want to get married with me. My godmother gladly answered, *"Why did you choose her? She is not pretty? You can find somebody else prettier than her anybody out there."* Mr. Fred said, *"No, no, no. She is pretty to me and I really love her very much. I really love her and both my parents like her very much.* That's why I came over here in Badian to propose marriage to her."

Mr. Fred offered a delicious pastry to my godmother; homemade from his mother to share with my parents in Badian. Then my godmother was already thinking that it's better that they go to our house so they can all share the delicious pastries to everybody in the family since there are plenty. These were the most delicious pastries delicacy ever, called *bodbod in the Visayan region.* Mr. Fred met Miss Silvano's mom and dad. Surely, they went to my house right across by the road and by the way, we were in the same neighborhood within that community.

My parents were very surprised about his visit. Mr. Fred introduced himself to my parents and asked them, *"Where is Miss Silvano?"* My parents said, *"She went to the city to follow up on some paper works."* My parents asked him, *"What is your reason why you're asking for her?"* Mr. Fred answered, *"I wanted to really respectfully tell you, Mr. and Mrs. Silvano. I really love your daughter, and I want to marry her. This is the reason for my visit. "We already had a good talk with her back then at the school, in Tanjay College, and by the way, I am also a teacher at Tanjay Elementary School; that's the beginning of my acquaintance with her."* My father asked Mr. Fred a question, *"How come you came here without her knowing that you are coming?"* Mr. Fred answered, *"This was just to attempt to communicate with each one of us. And I want to have a proof in saying to see is to believe.*

Most of these ideas and thoughts are my original thoughts and the interpretation of my love for her. *Ever since she left, I think of her every day, but I can't help falling in love with her. So I just decided to come."* Mr. Fred's parents agreed to him for his visit to Badian, and they said to him; *to stay out of trouble. Follow the golden rule, do everything that everybody else expected you to do, that will allow you to maximize your potential and to enjoy your love life to the fullest.*

Mr. Fred realized that he was not doing any good by forcing himself to go to our home and relating his love life as unfortunate bad luck. He certainly wasn't inspired by the visit. I knew he felt fear and embarrassed with my parents. By the end of the day, the result had become more and more desperate and the experience of his love life was a major challenge for Mr. Fred, who was feeling disheartened and depressed. He spent about four hours at my house waiting for me to return, but I did not arrive on time. I didn't know that he was there.

At around 3:00 p.m., Mr. Fred asked my parents that he wanted to go home already. Mr. Fred was really, really very disappointed about his visit. He told my parents to tell me about his visit and that he will come back next time, *"and please let her know that she is the brightest star in my future."*

Mr. Fred drove me crazy.

I didn't know what the answer was, so do not ask me anymore because I'm still trying to figure it out what the answer should be. I have to be able to know;

Arithmetic and the four fundamentals of mathematic which are "Addition, Subtraction, Multiplication, and Division"

If I was wrong! Oh well! Life goes on!

"Even though I'm the only one who feels this way"

I'm just only a simple woman, my heart and mind has the power of human imagination, this love of mine is qualified in deceiving any and every level of love. Remember, only your own decision and knowledge of your love lifestyle can protect you from being under control.

Indeed, silence is always better than meaningless words, but it is also difficult to comprehend the love and make a decision that would haunt me for the rest of my existence. Mr. Fred has the idea of instant success in his love, and the key to determine was that he would win. But he was very disappointed for his visit in my beautiful place in Badian during that time.

Mr. Fred listened to the beat of his heart and mind, his hope and inspiration will come true. To tell you the truth you will never become successful by dreaming; you have to do much in action, far beyond, to reach goals of love. He had to make sure and take action of himself.

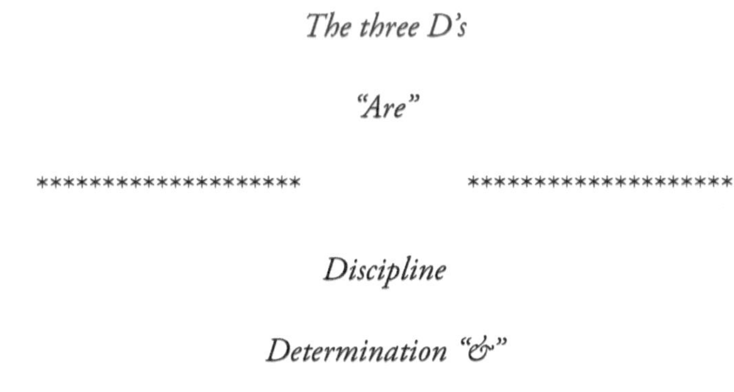

The three D's

"Are"

*******************   ******************

Discipline

Determination "&"

Desire

The three D's are important. This foundation will enable you to face the challenge and effort to overcome your love life excitement for an extended period of time, and appear to remember Mr. Fred is embarking on a new love lifelong journey that will last forever because he was too afraid that our unlovable will end a bad love relationship, too nervous about getting hurt, too sensitive to criticism and to speak out the true love.

He treasured everything that we talked about before. He said: *to see is to believe.* This kind of testimony of his love was faithfully infused in his thoughts with emotion and truth. That's why he came to my place in Badian without my knowing because he wanted to fulfill his promises to me.

It was the hardest moment ever. His words are still never forgotten till today. There is so much more to remember. So that I can see he is really telling the truth, *to see is to believe.* The detail and repetition of his thoughts all of a sudden he was falling in love that caused his anxiety to come into his love life happy and put your foot upon the neck of the fear of criticism.

Do not forget, Mr. Fred was not in it yet. So make sure you identify your goal first in your love life before focusing on your desire. In return, his love and determination led him to go to Badian; and took pride in it with his own discipline.

He wasn't afraid of the heightened love and the consequences of loving. My friendship with Fred is not only a one time deal but a special friendship that I'll forever cherish.

"You are the salt of the earth, but if the salt loses its flavor, how shall it be seasoned? It is then good for nothing but to be thrown out and trampled underfoot by men." (Matthew: 5:15) Truthful love shall be established forever, but a lying love is hot for a moment and will fizzle out later on.

It was a wonderful experience when I realized that love became all the faith I ever knew. From that time on, I did not see him anymore. Little did I know that this would be a relationship that would last forever, I know that this Mr. Fred watched the rest of the present time lovers being opened thinking there's something he needed to do. He just decided to come to Badian without my knowing; he just couldn't quite figure out what to do. Or maybe it was not that bad after all.

His decision gave him the best idea and hope with more of a bereaved type part of his love lifestyle. He wondered why and how he could ever get over with his falling in love with me. He loved me from the bottom of his heart, he said. And that is why he dedicated a song for me entitled, *"I can't stop loving you my dear, I always love you."* Each one of us has a personal belief in ourselves to follow like the road of success, and the satisfaction of our love life to follow our dreams. It is only to the extent that we find the courage to walk our own path of life, truly effective at peace with a purpose.

"Just like the example about the boat"

"*We want our boat in the water but we don't want the water in our boat, because if the water is inside our boat, the boat will sink.*" One day, I'm truly concerned over my shock. I received a letter from Josh in Hawaii and that he will come back for vacation in the Philippines.

Again for the second time, something shocking happened to me. I was invited by my girlfriend of mine to attend a beautiful welcome party for her uncle Josh from abroad. We shook hands for the second time with each other I looked up to him. I took that long nice right hand, and looked up into those deep brown eyes and I felt really impressed by him.

As we were sitting down in the chair, he told us his stories about the travels in the Philippines, and I remembered listening to him as we have our conversation and he said; "My long journey was to be a proud moment indeed. I'm ready to harvest this young beautiful woman I have wanted before."

I looked at him and we laughed, and I just ignored what was said.

He seemed to like me, I glanced slightly, and my heart pondered, but I have a negative feeling because he is older than me. Then I just continued entertaining him. He played his guitar and sang songs to me and I sang songs to him too. And I was asking questions about Hawaii. He has a genuine honest answer about him. He said he is pure single, he has never married before. He does not have any girlfriend. He doesn't smoke. He won't drink any alcoholic thing. He does not gamble and he will watch movies sometimes if he wants to during weekends by himself.

He enjoyed going to work every day.

His life was practically busy. He was the youngest in a family of two. His older sister married already and his dad passed away when Josh was young. He lived together with his mom until she passed away. If I have ever been threatened by failure of something I want, chances are my feelings of love will be broken. Love is like a flower for all seasons. Imagine, *it's been said that love has many ways of saying that love is a many splendor thing. Love is blind and lovers cannot see, near or far, wherever you are.*

I believe that the heart does go on, and once more you open your heart and you are in love and my heart will go on. I believe that there are some loved that will never go away. They were all smart and handsome. There were much more to remember when I looked at them. You do not know which one will be the best lifetime lover. You do not know who will be able to hold the right star that shines till the end of time.

Yet love is blind but lovers cannot see. I have discovered that I am not pretty or beautiful, but I knew and honestly believed that all of the books approved that I looked prettier to all the man who loved me before in my time. Happy lovers have learned to think enthusiastically if you aren't fired with enthusiasm.

The most important part of my success came from: *trials, troubles, and truth believing it,* even as I worked hard and the proof is seen in my hands. Something caught my eye when I looked closer at each of their pictures. My love life was not easy to explain. What happened to my enticing love life?

Too sensitive to speak out, my love life was about a string of moments in time. But it still amazes and wondered if those were how everyone's lovers interact. I thought sometimes love is many miracles, powerful you might imagined, there are some loved that will not go away.

My compassionate love has given the care and all loving concern. It wasn't entirely true that I didn't have time to fall in love, but I was trapped in an unwanted situation, too afraid of awakening my emotions. Too nervous about getting serious loving and promising each other is not good especially, I know in my heart, I'm not serious to both of them and I know, I am still comparing for all of them.

I almost thought that all of my dreams would come true. Well, I thought that I am running out of time, I mean just let go of something you love, that love is like a wheel of fortune game, when you hit the right one then you win. There is no scale to weigh the equivalence of love. It is measured by your own desire. Like the first butterfly that pollinated the flowers, sometimes when a bird approaches the butterflies, the poor butterflies fly away and so, butterflies missed the beautiful flowers.

Love is just a gamble, the key to receiving the riches of love lies in our willingness to accept them to love and to be love. Then what you are about to read was the real love stories that happened to my love life indeed. If you continue reading until the end of this book then you will know how to choose the person who you really love. Use your brains and not your heart. You know my girlfriend said, *"My uncle Josh will visit her in the Philippines and that we want you to be the lovers love of him, what? I said; are you kidding me?* She laughed, and said; because you are the best majority chosen by our family's eyes. It seemed I'm confused, I felt was causing my current love like clouds and wind without rain. I lived the hills above the road in a beautiful secure place community. I am proud to say I have a couple boyfriends to choice I did not pick them they pick me, but no serious relationships. I know my choice was so hard, but no decision had been made yet.

My sister whispered to me, *"Don't take too long in choosing among them. Be practical just choose the dollars not the pesos."* I simply nodded to my sister and I sat for a long time without speaking. I wondered what my sister was thinking but I'm sure she was thinking of the good things that would happen in the future of my life.

"For I was hungry and you gave me food; I was thirsty and you gave me drink; I was a stranger and you took me in." (Matthew 25:35)

After over a year, Josh made a surprise visit at my house. He played his guitar and sang songs to me and I also sang songs to him. He chose the meaningful songs about true love: *"Where Do I Begin."* We sang a couple songs until he was about to go home. As we continued to share our stories with each other, I was inspired and happy. After listening to his story, I have found out that we have a lot of things in common.

I knew Joshua was a positive thinker. In fact, he just threw words to me saying, "I want to settle down at this time. I've enough traveling and I was very happy I chose to come to the Philippines and this is it. But I wasn't paying attention to his story because he was being so direct and telling these things the first time we met.

After all I have other hidden lovers on the other side of the road. So I did not react at that time. He spent fifteen days' vacation in the Philippines and back home to Hawaii on time. It was a big surprise in my part which I thought, he will just forget all those things but instead, he sent me a letter with dollars inside to buy me a uniform.

So I replied to him, *"Thank you for those dollars you sent to me. I am really happy."* I treasured everything Josh sent me, but this kind of letters with dollars on it was one of my favorites. Just kidding, Anyway, I bought three sets of school teacher's uniform for me accessories that made me feel very sophisticated. I took a photograph and sent it to him as a kind of testimony with pure thoughtfulness and love.

At the back of the photograph I had written, "The image of this uniform gave me strength and a sense of being very special." Love life started to get to me. We send and correspond through letters once in a. I was not able to write as much as I could because I was too busy at the classroom and he said he was busy too with his job at McBryde Sugar Company.

His job was a machine operator and that he didn't have time to take a vacation any more until the next two years. Not much but he knew, he sent me a letter again it all figured out. I read a couple more; he would always say I love you. "I love you more and more each day, I wake up in the morning and I wonder, I hope everything is the same. I think of you when I was there in the Philippines; we have shared together our acquaintances about love story.

There were too much to remember our lifetime of memories. *So I'm telling you wait for me, my darling.* I will come back to get married to you, but to put it into words, I do not know if I am able to hold you, I am not there every day and yet this love of mine is needed to fully express the way I feel in love about you.

Between those two years, I took an honest look at my love life." However, I find it hard solving my problems, because I can see Josh. He was a big man with a heart to match. I watched the world outside meeting him for the first time brought me to the scene. What shall I do with those inner beings who quite in love with me. I'm not ready to commit to anybody yet. I don't want to carry out destruction without a good thought. Even these must be given a choice through one in which my love life can be contained.

The most powerful requirement of love, takes courage, self confidence and trust to go through hurtful feelings and stay in love with who the best or you want the most. Stay with my thinking that my love could hold him. The greatest need on the love relationships is the path of truth. The good memories of yesterday's journey is tomorrow's destiny, what a beautiful and meaningful thought, he was doing what he enjoyed, what makes him feels good, what makes him happy.

The happiest and most contented individuals are those who, each day, perform to the best of their ability, and follow their dreams remembered I hadn't slept well, when waking after my every dream. It's such a good feeling coming over me, as if verifying the passages of time that my dreams would come true. This special moment wondering in most everything I see, it was not in doing what, I do not liked but in liking what I do, that was the secret of my happiness Dr. Bob was on his vacation here in our own town fiesta celebration. I have seen him, that was how I know, what especially for me, and the reason was clear. It's because he was here a matter of finding myself and building upon what I have found.

But before I forget, I have to acknowledge to my other hiding lovers Joshua, Fred and Lloyd were they around my thought, how can I forget them here will stay in my thought forever. But at that point in time, I must learn to forget and I try to change my expectation level of love.

I think everyone has the secret I must have a strong belief in myself and my goals of love. But Dr. Bob and I have been acquainted since we were teenager because we were neighbor. I mean, do we know each other well? Of course, I know him. Looking back, I found out that we were schoolmates when we were elementary school. There was beauty when you live in the same community, remembering, and wondering about the friendship, and little by little we were able to get to know and like each other better, and eventually became lovers.

Believe it or not

I knew that everybody else wants to see it before they believe it, but I must keep it a secret. Believe it or not, it is true. Love care was so important we all shared the greatest journey of love lifestyle self-awareness within us who are. *Compassionate, precious, loving and kind, perhaps, true love lasts forever who was extremely in love will wait to fertilize the flowers in the garden of thoughts and watering the seeds.* Before I even see it or doing it, so that I have more faith in my own power of love I should really believe that I can reach my own potential desire. Everything starts with believing before seeing at least we kept our promises. In getting more of what you want is to ask for such blessing what you already have, and you can ask for more love.

Simply I set my mind of what I wanted, and then allow the information that will enable me to be happy. Without stress and without problems to be sure would come through, and do not give too much weight to the dictation from my heart of being in love of whatever I do, as I said before, if ever say when I fall in love, I must study first do not follow my heart, follow my mind, think, before *I say I do.* Dr. Bob sang a song dedicated to be highly internal his own ability and control events, to make things happen, and because he believe that, he actively make things happen he knew his own destiny, to keep his mind clear and balanced, his fashion was as natural.

For me as it would be for a butterfly trying as to fly as high to reach the sky.

This reminds me of an occasion in terms of at least two ways: *first an incident and second a result.* To be nobody but your self; nothing in this world wide let for me to see, and I'm doing its best night and day, to make me just liked everybody else, and that means to fight the greatest battle of my love life and there was to fight and never stop fighting until somebody will win, love demands attention of the true love that distinguishes the greatness of love from the bottom of our heart, and that' how to succeed in love.

The memories of your
love is forever

Love is what our thoughts make it a memory, the memories is usually the fruit of intelligent application. To touch me with all my heart all apart there, now ends forever, be smart together, to fight our love, to be a winner in the game.

You're memories made me realize this was our love life hoping they understand the love life result. Basically we were not hiding our love life result, our recollection was hiding in your mind what if, and we can see the picture. Then our memory were consequences it becomes a love life story, be smart enough to begin this study as early in our love life as possible.

This road map shows us of how to find out exactly our destination where we want to go. If we follow our direction, we have the ability and the opportunity to be highly successful. This result we can succeed if we follow our minds decision to take responsibility for our self, and if we believe that our love life will be success.

It was just a matter over our love appear which we have completed control. The rules of love life are very simple it will become familiar with everybody, in every minute, every hour, everyday, every week, every month, and every year.

Then study them follow them, don't ever give up on them, eventually, we will creates all the success we really want to win in our love life. Dr. Bob said; we don't have to be sick to get better, our love life plan should covered these area was worth more than leaving success and realization of a worthy ideal.

The moment right before summer 1975 the department of education had transferred me to another school at Madredejos High School Bantayan Island. I must have it, this is what it is, I hold and cherish my dreams. Like the rivers of education better than all the waters of love, for man his days are like grass as a flower of the field, so he flourishes for the wind passes over it and it was gone. Instead of the forgotten dreams my love from the bottom of my heart's desire will recognize love.

Summer break classes 1975, was approaching the director of the public school superintendent send me a big brown envelope instructed me to transfer to other school at Madredejos High School. I opened the enveloped to be sure to emphasize that the subject was for me, surely, enough my name was printed in a big letter in front of the form that confirming definite transfer to Madredejos High School this summer break class 1975.

Rather I sending Mr. Fred a letter to inform about the subject, instead, my student told him ahead of time, that I'm transferring to teach to another school. How strange it sounded to, he already knew, it had been supposed to be a very long love stories and hard to begin with, but, it becomes very short and simple. There was no less painfully and there had been the days, weeks, and months of dealing with Mr. Fred that emotionally interesting conversation, and he was eager to marry me. But, my first thought it was just like a triangle love, they were three each the same side.

There were no other moments dedicated to who I have to be getting married yet, no names listed in my mind and maybe soon all will be forgotten. However, wouldn't it be great to looked into the mirror every morning and say to myself, I am the best lover to who I could love, and no one in this planet is going to spoil my love life for me, I could not persuade my own self. I knew that I'm not pretty, or beautiful, but, I have very positively believed, that I could be the best partner choice or beautiful to all the man who love me before. I mean things you could change, your real dreams. If you have no passion, there was no excitement, but in those days relationships there were no offered in a romance interest, maybe just get lucky if you could really made one trick pony. At the precise moment even if you've knew each other already, you could bowed down your head ever so slightly asked permission if you could hold my hand also things to talk about. As for me, I felt more than that it doesn't seem to know that confident part of our self as well as we used to, would really reach to the North Pole if you really want to.

Winter 1975 class season soon to begin and I am getting ready to go home for preparation a quick boat ride for me to go home in Cebu where I live. Perhaps, in the last couple of weeks, I will be leaving again to other island where I am going to teach there. I had done a few clean up already. I missed my students and I loved all them, they all liked me. I enjoyed teaching them especially in mathematic. So my time was up, I'm pretty sure I will remember them.

I went home for my summer vacation. In spite of the moving to other school, I must go to the University of the Visayas first to attend a summer class for my master degree to become a high school principal. Then I will continue later for the next summer which I almost done, I have nine more units to finish my master degree. So, I was just too busy during that time. I went home first then I am headed on the next week to my new assignment at Madredejos high school.

It was a new adventure for me, new places, new students, new school, new friends, looks like new everything for me. I started with new beginning again, and I still have to go beyond my own understanding and make changes to improve the world. Being active in seeking virtue was of the utmost important expressing my love life. But I do not have to do it now, just leave it alone. I started getting to know my new students their getting familiar with me, and I getting familiar with them too. They were nice to me after all I enjoyed my life teaching over there.

I started getting to know many friends. So, if I just make my own ideas enough to expose my self to their thinking and put their ideas into action these principles will lead me to everything I wanted to do. Patience was the companion of wisdom, it was not easy how to do, but I can say, I'm being successful coming over here to teach and I met some nice people. Relationships are not measured in time but in lessons learned.

Looking back, I am surprised with my love life passion because sometimes it's too complicated, I have four choices. I even regret it now. My dreams brings great sleeping beauty to my love life, but also great sadness, and I'm not sure it's a fair exchange for someone true love. Someone should enjoy the other things if they can, they should spend their days in the sun. But mine was always spent by reading and writing my lesson plan.

After everything was in place a surprised as anyone I could imagine. If days were pleasant, the evening times grew increasingly tense. An excitement I had to learn a normal tradition culture a town fiesta held and celebration at Madredejos Bantayan Island. It was so happen all the teachers were invited to the festival. All teachers must attend the event.

It was required by the mayor in town it was part of the support from the school.

As we were there at the tennis court, I asked myself, *who am I? And how, I wonder, I thought of it, will this dancing be a good one?* Or it was worth waiting, while we were sitting with our groups, there was one table assigned just for all of us only high school teachers. I'll never know what made everything feel was on my face I can't hide myself there was a man wanted to dance with me that night with his very own inspiration.

The announcer guy announce and introduce us to the public that we were the high school teachers attending this festival and he thanks to all of us for attending that evening event. Again was somebody had just came out of the blue, and he introduced himself, *hi, my name is Lloyd*, we shook hands with each other, he said, he just arrived from Cebu City to attend that festival celebration.

He knew that there is a new teacher transfer from the other island, that was the news of the town, and he really wanted to see that person, and that was me. His nice curly hair and outfit were perfect. He is tall and handsome and spook idly with flattering lips and a double heart he speaks.

He studied at the University of the Visayas for his engineering course. And that he almost done with his engineering career, I looked at him for a moment more and then glanced back at him, he was tall and heavy-set with a handsome face, nice curly hair good looking guy. He looked at me with new interest, and he asked me to dance with him, I said, alright and as we were dancing together, we talked story, the attraction was natural mutual and immediate very strong intention. *He said, now we were more than acquainted to each other, our conversation was very intuitive talented and full of attention, tell me now, do you have a boyfriend? I spook slowly to answer and I'm thinking of my three hiding love, Josh, Bob, and Fred. What happen to my enticing love story, and what it was all about? Thoroughly to teach your self in love with somebody is the best way to learn for your thought with long lasting memory.*

Somewhere my love

Somewhere over the rainbow, where is the rainbow, my answer said, *I don't know what you're talking about. He laughed, and said, you mean you don't know anything? You don't know anything about flying bird either?*

I said; no, I'm not thinking of flying bird right now, no bird flies at night, we will see about that, if there is any, only those birds are awake, they flies looking for something about different things because birds are very intelligent.

He had not taken his eyes off me, and so, we continued dancing through the night until the celebration was finished. He watching me every moved I made, his attention be attracted to the last place on earth.

I wanted to walk out of the dancing place. But I stumbled down, waiting for my co-teachers to go home. That was the hardest thing I had ever knew at the sound of music his in front of me wanted to dance, and he wouldn't asked another girl to dance but me.

I predicted maybe this will be another boyfriend again, to correct that I would not answer him. The question he asked me. I was thinking but there was no tie to undo about it, so just let it go. Like the first waves which tightly encircle in the stone, everything in our lives was connected with love.

You will never forget the hurt, but as time passes you can handle to live around it. Success is like getting what you want, happiness was those wanting what you get, and that was the reward for a good accomplishment, something you love to do and be the very best at doing it. It was the next week Monday I was ready to go to school, I heard walking sounds as I was about to open the door. It was him. He laughed and looked at me. He said, *"Good morning, Miss Silvano." I answered,*

"Good morning, Mr. Lloyd, how are you?"

He said fine. But I never know that he has a love letter with him. We were walking together on the way to school but it was not a far distance, it's only across the road where my boarding house was. We were talking as we were walking, and then when we had almost reached the school, Lloyd handed his love letter to me secretly. We shook hands again.

He said, "Thank you for the dance from the other night." "You are welcome, Mr. Lloyd."

I knew the feeling and the thoughts of him consumes me, and I would focus instead on meeting the expectations to whom I love. He was just anxious as if nothing could hold him back. I could feel him looking at me, he said, "I'm only trying to let you know that what I feel is true.

It's like no matter what I do, for the first time I saw you, I really fell in love with you." "Oh, my goodness, Mr. Lloyd, hold on to it."

I thought it was my first and foremost responsibility to tell him, "Don't ask me because I'm trying to figure out and I don't know what's down the road."

Afternoon came, I went home for lunch. I opened Mr. Lloyd's love letter and read, he said, *"You were the treasure that I was longing to find. Without your love I could be lost."*

I knew the afternoon was coming to an end he came to the school and was watching me when I'd be ready to go home because he wanted to walk with me. His warm big smile began to form on his lips that made his love life worth precious to me for a while. I tried not to pay attention to what he said because I don't want to disturb my concentration on my classes.

I knew beyond any doubt that he was becoming in love with me. He could not take his eyes off me that night when he danced with me. I looked at his brown eyes and his nice thick eyebrows. I noticed it instantly his hand grasped to hold me and maybe on his mind, he knew it would be the shook of electricity touched his heart in the flesh being awakened by his current love life. He say's you're beautiful trail's me off and I knew, I seen a signs for that moment he fall in love with me.

Lloyd give me a side looked from his right eye, with much passion way and I knew right away his feeling liked a raging river's flows. He does not know what to do still trying to figure it out.

His mind flashed back to the Saturday evening only a few months earlier when I just arrive. He knew there's one new teacher at high school just arrived, and that he wants to meet that teacher very soon. And that was me, how could it be that this was not a simple pleasure. I don't want to meet anybody anymore because I'm too occupied. I intend to work hard as a teacher. It was my responsibility to teach my students to learn about certain subjects. And my every intention is to be totally responsible for my love life and I promised to myself that I don't want to allow myself to fall in love with somebody else and I don't want to make any mistakes.

I believe I am not what I have, and I am not what I do. All the rest of love life's miracles would never be treasured and suddenly, I am competent in my career to enjoy my life profession and my relationship with people. I have a good intention to have a positive expectation to have a successful outcome. I don't want that Mr. Lloyd struck his face like a sweet honey and will steal my heart completely.

I see the lights in the wheel of fortune game hijacking all the eyes of the people passing by, hoping they eager to bit and they can make the lucky surprise winning prizes. The winners in life will always think they were constantly lucky in terms of *I can, I must, I will, and I am.*

Otherwise the losers, on the other hand, they always concentrate in their waking thoughts on what they are supposed to have and they should have done to win the prizes or what they were not supposed to do it.

Early in the summer 1976, the class season was going to an end. I went home for my summer vacation, at the same time I continued my master's degree at the University of the Visayas in Cebu City. After the last few weeks, I had learned that my faraway friend Josh has arrived in Badian where I lived, But I didn't bother because I stayed in the city to continue my studies, *because I need to be more smarter than I am.* I wanted to concentrate to achieve my goal of success. I did the best I could with studying and my intention that by finishing and practicing the principles of education, I will be able to achieve all my real world and willingness to turn into success and have the freedom and responsibility to choose being where I intend to live in my life.

Each one of us has a destiny in love, and it was only when we believe in ourselves that we can have it. Success is a journey treasure and not a destiny procedure. Now that a year had passed, I usually teach in schools, going from island to island. *Well, I don't think I was really serious about love. I mean, give me a break, he's far away from me. I sure hope that dreams come true; it's too good to be true.*

Afternoon came, when I went home at my boarding place, my landlord was an old acquaintance of my parents. They were close friends. She told me to go home to Badian right away because Josh wanted to see me. *"He just arrived from Hawaii and he is here to marry you," She said to me with a curious expression.* I am very proud of my landlord for her love of my family she has given to me. She talked to me with the tears coming out from her eyes—flood of happiness and unconditional love. Love is complete acceptance when two people allow their love exactly as they are without any belief of love for each other.

The secret of success is to accomplish the best that you can do and think of everything that almost anything, I did not forget about whether I might win or lose, and by doing so, I was working hard, and practicing my skills that I really love. I wanted to set the records about my life. I never entertained any lovers that have come to my life before, or any offer about love story.

"I know love can wait if you are willing to pay the price."

Life is what the mind's love can conceive, and it can be achieve by believing it. The problem was, some individuals do not set goals of their love life in the first place. I did not have much trouble achieving my own goal, some have delighted themselves with love and have gone on a very long journey and will come on the appointed day.

It has been said that the everlasting love go a long period of time without speaking, and never question came the intruder of the beginning initiation of the enticing love life stories. That to be sure, it's too good to be true, and a fantasized shining love abroad, and will become a true dream and the inspiration of your love.

An individual lover's love abroad, plus there are three others that their love relationships were better pretend, it isn't easy to do. Those lovers pick up their phone like they just spoke yesterday, regardless of how long it has been, or how far away they live and they don't hold grudges.

They understand that the world was mine, and can't be theirs, my love, so why should they pretend. Our lives were very busy and they always love her/him. Those lovers knew who they are. They both were handsome they have their own values in their love life, motives, and their complete acceptance. *Bob, Fred, Josh, and Lloyd* leaving a long lasting good impression, they follow their dreams, and they will not be afraid to go back, and stand under that one red flower, and walk straight ahead to their own destination.

Whatever the minds of the individuals can be conceived and believed, it can achieve love. Thoughts and powerful things when mixed with the definiteness of love and burning desire, the determination of love that whether you are loved or not loved, you did the best indeed. Do your best every day and your love life will gradually expand into satisfying fullness condition.

If you are really in love to somebody, you will never find another love to anybody. But you must understand this very important fact maybe you are just kidding your love life or yourself. *A simple advice for lovers: do not mistake excitement as love, the first time it appears, you must make time for it, find time to evaluate, find time to really, really understand it. Whoever wasted time to find it, has not discovered the value of love life?*

Remember, great things have no fear of time and love. *Do not agree to any offer, think first of what is good before you say yes, follow your dreams, do not follow your heart, but follow your mind; think and evaluate first what is good. Oh, my goodness again*, I said to my landlord, "What should I do?" She said, "Let's go to Badian together and find out what will happen, because if you will not go home to Badian, Josh will come over here, and that I am afraid if Lloyd knew about the news, and he would come to my house too. I don't want that to happen that way, two of them would come to my place. And I don't want you to go home alone." *My landlord knew all about tentatively there was a problem when we reached in Badian because all the people talked and that they would spread the news in the small town.*

My landlord and I, arrived in Badian and she told my parents about what would be going to happen. The best thing and wisest idea is to let Josh and Daria get married already, so it will be done and confirmed, everybody in the family, a reason for expressing the marriage is to overcome the hassle of the problem to come.

We should avoid the trouble especially, for Josh he wasn't too familiar and experienced of every thinking mind. This is very sacred marriage and we must act right away before Lloyd learn of what we are doing, because he can take over Josh's place. He is here in Badian already with his two army friends.

First and foremost it happened I was so scared on one time when Lloyd came to Badian along with his two army friends in uniform with the rifle too. *He asked, "Why? What happened to my beloved; she was hijacked by someone who's from abroad."* The path was very straight as ever, but now it all strewn with the rocks and gravel that should accumulate over a long period of time.

"I saw no reasons when I observed Josh, ready to get married already."

On Saturday, May 4, 1976, Josh and his relatives came to my house to talk to my parents. He wanted to get married with me. *"Oh my goodness."* I'm just telling these things, *if it's to be, it's up to me,* and I have to skip from the ordinary way, isn't it fun to have a hidden love from abroad?

After all, you got to go abroad? My landlord wondered. Her determination and commitment will cause you to be any other way but looked at all your lovers, and *you should choose the dollar instead of pesos. My landlord said, and my sister whispered to me too, and said, "Just choose the dollar not the pesos.* I was dragging to myself to make a conscious decision and who I would be willing to get married and love the most, but I just used my brains to determine the best choice. Like I said previously, when choosing your love life, do not follow your heart, but follow your mind.

So I did. I made my way from the troubled water onto the edge of the hijacking airplane later. I must make a final decision soon because majority wins, my beliefs, I had accomplished most of what I had wanted to do. I made a final decision, *I chose the dollar instead of the pesos.* That was Josh's vision wanted to see the beauty of his dreams eager to come to the Philippines and wanted to settle in a marriage in a simple beginning.

The content of my life the choices I had made was incongruent with who I'm going to be with. I was too occupied with Bob, Fred, Lloyd, and Josh. I realized that it was a different feeling, this love for me, one that I never expected but, looking back, I supposed it couldn't have ended those love in another way. My parents wanted the simple truth from me. They wanted that I choose the love that I have taken, a love that pleases a lot of my family and friends most of them with good intentions, but not me simply because the majority wins.

"That made the evening news on how to succeed in love."

Unfortunately, exciting news came along. Lloyd arrived in Badian too, with his two army friends in uniform with rifles looking for me (where was my house), he then asked the driver of the bus where was my house exactly. Then finally, he found my house. I wondered whether Josh and I would hide somewhere else, and for that matter my entire family felt as uneasy as I did. I told myself maybe nothing really upsetting was going to happen that time. He went inside my house together with his companions, and my parents invited my godmother if she could come to my house and help them entertain Lloyd.

Everyone was on their best behavior. There were plenty of news in town, I didn't want to show myself to him at all. I was terrified by the stories I heard of that Lloyd wanting to fight with Josh. Lloyd said, according to the news, "If I can't have her, no one can, no one will hijack her." Lloyd said, "I came over here in Badian to get married to her." In spite of all that had happened, Josh and I were too terrified still, fighting for strength and a sense of being safe. My heart skipped a beat, frightened that made me feel what if Lloyd could see us walking under the coconut tress with my landlord toward Josh's relative's house, and if he would know that we were there hiding from Lloyd, then he can pull the trigger. I paused for just a moment, thinking of the whole situation.

He came over here in Badian at this time to meet me and my parents, but unfortunately he never saw me at all. My godmother and my parents entertained Lloyd at my house. They sat down in the chairs together and they talked to each other. He was not able to meet me, and it was very disappointing on his part.

An important move such visit I wish upon no one. Josh and I had evacuated to Josh's relative's house. I thought obviously worried about Lloyd, he was unable to talk or see me at all for he was wildly jealous of my relationship with Josh from abroad. His expression said, please give me a chance, I will find her if I will stay here in Badian for a while, all it takes was listened and asked people's talked.

He was so disappointed about his coming, and he hate his visit in Badian. He said, *"I hated myself for getting so deeply in love with her, I'm sorry but that's the truth." Imagine that every thought my godmother thinks, she whispered to Lloyd, "Are you really falling in love with her?" "Of course!" "Yes?" He said, "I love her very much. I know that she is the most beautiful woman in the world for me. Every word I utter, and every feeling I experience will automatically magnetize her name and more for her picture." "Why did you choose her? She is not pretty enough, and you can find somebody prettier than her some place out there." He feels like a fool, but you're asking me, and so I'm telling you. He said, "I always love her."*

A moment later, tears flowed down his cheeks; he tried is best to keep his tears away. He nodded and left the house at that moment of grief and sorrow; Lloyd tried his best. He felt sorry for himself . . . a lifetime of his memories of his love now end forever, and he said, "I thought I will be your man, my love. I do not know if I am able to live without you. I remember you and how you were then, beautiful to me.

I dream of all the time, and wounded with the hurt that will come when something very special is taken away from my heart." Everybody and all my friends in town were much alert. I stood up after a good reluctant pause I don't want to meet him at all. My friends and the neighborhood were all watching him and what was going to happen next. I was hiding in Josh's relative's house. I stood up by the window looking down the road where Lloyd and his two army companies with rifles in their shoulders standing there under the monkey pod tree. I was afraid and be very afraid, if he would know I was there at that house right next to him standing there. Lloyd looking absolutely wonderful and handsome, exactly the way he was when I left the island at Madridejos High School a year ago. I thought to myself, I haven't seen to myself eye to eye on everything. I'm not perfect or beautiful, but, I did the best I could.

According to the books I have read, and agree that I have looked and more beautiful to all the men who had loved me before. I kept thinking, what should I do to assure me the truth and figure out something better for me to say something easier to think about at first, the world would not be able to withstand my heartache. I was afraid of myself being too troubled and terrified to imagine the love life.

Evening came. They were unable to return home after all. They stayed at their relatives in our neighborhood in Badian, Cebu, Philippines. But still, I was not feeling right. It was just very frightening and romantic to think that being true hiding love burned into my mind forever had proved to be an incredibly liberating love experience for me. What happened to my enticing love story?

The sun has come up shining a bit, and the rainbow appeared by my window like a dream of many colors with a bright orange, yellow, green, red, and blue; and I hope that it will never go away. I made a right decision straight from the heart.

Love is the key and whenever there's *a majority rule, majority wins*. I can simply choose Josh because he was what the majority voted for— by the whole family, but my heart dreadfully answered: whatever will be, will be. That means just follow your dreams.

Remember when despite my own acceptance it still amazes me, it's not easy to ignore, and to say the magic words I love you but it was impossible now to guide the entire universe, and you and I were a part of it. My love life choices I had made were incongruent with who I'm going to be with. I was too occupied with *Bob, Fred, Lloyd, and Josh.*

After many correspondences, he returned to the Philippines in May 1976 to marry me. He returned to Hawaii alone, and made a petition for me to come and join him in Hawaii. You know, failures want pleasing methods, success wants pleasing results, love wants pleasing loving. The train of failure usually runs on the type of laziness. You must take control of your love.

There was one moment in time that the secret of a dream bumped their way down the road of my love and gave me the strength and a sense of being very special. It was not discouraged by failure, but, it can be a positive love life experience. It was in my heart and stayed alive every time, and I must take time to enjoy the moment. My love life has been the attempt to give a picture in a road map of happiness that brings the same joy and satisfaction in my everyday life.

I have to make sure my dreams are the greatest influence in my love life decisions and activities. It should be the focus of my love life, which does not get better by hope; it gets better by a plan if given enough time to understand the meaning of *LOVE*. That's why, I have faced the big solution with anticipation, and I got excited by following my dreams in advance when I have designed my future results about the enticing love story of mine.

Monday, May 4, 1976. Josh and I got express marriage by a mayor at the municipal hall in the town of Badian. Like an intimately close family and friends, then after that, the fear had become a part of me and it cannot be forgotten.

There's the original fear in my every thought and every action.

I am afraid to go out without thinking if Lloyd will kidnap me. I am afraid if Josh will get involved into fighting with somebody I know. I am afraid if I cannot fulfill my potential in life.

Tuesday, May 5, 1976. We got married again at the Catholic Church in Badian and that was a big wedding party. We invited our friends in town and relatives to attend the wedding. There were six sponsors at the wedding, my godparents, and Josh's relatives. That was the most unforgettable moment of my life.

The four hidden love stories begging to see me at least for the last time, power hungry to talk about our love stories and relationships. It was late in the afternoon and Josh liked to look at the reflections in the rivers called "SEMMA" and trees were beautiful in deep summer greens, yellows, and every shade in between. Josh said, "Look at the colors of those leaves.

It is like our relationship, its beauty is indescribable and unique.

In a week right after our marriage, Josh went back home to Hawaii and his returning ticket too expired on Friday afternoon.

So I had been powerfully forgetting all those hidden love of mine, my thought was influenced by my going abroad waiting for my visa to come. It takes seven months to get approval and finally. I came to Hawaii in February 1977.

Tears on My Pillow You don't remember me but I remember you. Give me a chance to succeed in love, my greatest weaknesses in love lies in not giving up. The most certain way to succeed is just to try some other time and can be as great as you want to be if you believe in yourself.

Over the years, I enjoyed living and continued my studies and worked my daily home routine, but our family was entirely different. As we start for the day my parents were very organized and disciplined. When it's time to work, we all do or everybody has to work. My sisters, brothers, and I were very busy with much more important things to do, and we helped our parents in whatever they were doing in the house. It was not at all a comfortable or easy life. But we care about our family and friends so much that we don't want to be anywhere else.

My parents were very strict, during my studies in the city, they wanted me to be successful. My parents said, "Make sure you focus on your studies!" because they don't know one school that teaches students how to be successful in love, or how to be happy, how to be self-accepting, and how students should have passion and take responsibilities for their own actions.

Customer imaginations profile:

I had a dream that enlightened me about going abroad. When I was a young teenager, I dreamed of going abroad but didn't know where.

I kept asking myself, *"What if I went to America? How would it look like over here in the Philippines?" According to my grandparents, all the people in America spoke in English. Then how could I speak in English when I did not know how to.* In my mind lay the thought of going to school so that I could learn how to speak in English. My parents did not permit me to continue my education because they could not afford to pay my education fees plus all the expenses of boarding house and allowances. So I decided to find my own source of income and I was lucky to find this couple who wanted to help me continue my education until I graduated from college.

I became a working student. I cooked for them, cleaned their house, and washed their clothes. I did everything—whatever they told me to do, I did it. It was as opportunity that I could either take or lose.

Finally, I finished my education. I became a teacher. I found my dream, and I wanted to follow my dream. I thought I could or couldn't, but either way, I would be correct in riding an airplane.

During that time, many of us young teenagers wanted to somehow migrate abroad. But I was the only one. I had to play my role in life as a gifted person. I found a pen pal who was willing to marry me. This is the starting point of my love life.

Josh and I got married on the Monday morning of May 4, 1976, at the mayor's office in Badian, Cebu, Philippines. We made it an express wedding because Lloyd arrived in Badian on the Sunday afternoon of May

3, 1976, to marry me at 7:00 p:m of the same day. So all my friends and relatives were alerted, and they hid me at Josh's cousin's house so that Lloyd could not find me. I was really scared.

Lloyd had two military friends who accompanied him that night; both of them had rifles in their hands, and they stayed overnight at their friend's house that evening. Josh and I ended up having two marriage contracts because we got married again in the Catholic Church in Badian, Cebu, Philippines, on May 5, 1976; at that time, we had a big celebration for our wedding. Most of my best friends, relatives, and neighbors attended the party.

One thing I cannot forget was that Josh was ready to fight against them, He said, "Who are these people? I can handle them one by one, but I don't want to be surprised." A love story ended in a fantastically successful marriage, a lover who take the time and trouble to develop themselves as lovers, who become excellent at their love, have the kind of security that lasts a lifetime; and that's how to succeed in love.

ADVICE!!!!!

1. Read as much as possible, don't limit yourself its author's has strengths and weaknesses.

2. Learn as much as you can about publishing, Learn how it works, how to get published, how to market your book, what editors look for. There's a wealth of information in any bookstore and it's important to understand the business aspects of writing.

3. You need to understand the conventions so-called commercial fiction, or is your goal simply to get published if so, write what you want, but write it well.

4. You cannot win a game if you don't play

5. And finally, write as much as you can, because you can't be a writer without writing.

6. You will find the courage to write experiment or any other

7. Unfortunately, the adults were anything BUT trustworthy

8. Take the courage, for example, wicked heart thrived on the teardrops of children.

9. Their very soul danced at the thought of crushing a child's spirit

10. They are dashing the hopes and dreams against the love

11. The jagged rocks of never-ending despair and loved

12. Everyday my dream would stand at my mind do this?

13. Gleefully handing out determination what to do next

14. My dream's enough to cross putrid path and for a very thought

15. The technique in writing you become famous is that write, write, write, as much as you can, that lets you animate the action! Don't give up. I don't care what's right or wrong, and I won't try to understand, let the devil take tomorrow, but let this book all will be done, yesterday was dead and gone, and tomorrow's out of sight, and it's sad this book to stop, help me make it through finish.

16. You make the difference between mediocrity and excellence

17. Think about it, upon finish of the book showing your name that will be placed in a book cover or anywhere of a book it is essential.

18. The more you think or need more than that even to think about strengthening our mindset standards of academic excellence is top.

19. Advantage mind a feeling of joy and pleasure in both reading and writing

20. Loved reading and writing about growing and learning together and the acceptance of mind can be the champion of your mind strength and the ability of the highest competence security.

www.ingramcontent.com/pod-product-compliance
Lightning Source LLC
Chambersburg PA
CBHW030352200726
48286CB00013B/1151